LOVE IN VENICE

MOLLIE MATHEWS

Blue Orchid
PUBLISHING

"I loved this story! *Love In Venice* leans toward the heart. Where love is the main character. Where you cheer for their relationship to flourish. There is one thing wrong with the story…I never wanted it to end. Honestly, I've never felt this way about a story before. Enjoy."

~ Jan Z.

"When workaholic Maggie is forced to take a vacation, She goes to Venice, first moment there and she is robbed, they take everything from her. Mauro is there to help her, too bad he is promised to another. What happens, when they realize that they have so much in common with each other. I loved this story."

~ Wioletta

"*Love In Venice* is a warmly romantic story set mainly in Venice. When Maggie and Mauro unexpectedly meet upon her arrival in Venice it was pure happenstance after she was robbed by gypsies. He comes to her rescue and she trusts him even when she's thinking, "What am I doing?" The characters have a depth to them and we peel back their layers a little at a time. She has her reasons for being in Venice, vacationing alone. I loved that their hearts seemed to speak to each other almost from their first meeting.

There is a wonderful flow to the story and beautiful and vivid descriptions of the city, his business and his home. Imagery was created throughout and I could envision myself in Venice - seeing the canal, the cobblestoned streets, the architecture and more. There are family and friends and lots of heart to heart moments between Maggie and Mauro.

He showed another side of himself to her that he normally keeps hidden and he's not himself even with the person he's promised to through a family arrangement. There is sadness and tears along with euphoria, loving, romance and love. There is also art brought in - both music and painting that touched their souls as well as mine.

There is a happily ever after that was portrayed better than I hoped. I love that we get to see how their lives unfold and the beautiful love they have for each other with the epilogue that really adds an additional layer to the story and brings in characters briefly whom we've met in other books. I love the detail of the cover.

Ms. Mathews is an author whose books I enjoy. She always transports me to someplace new with a cast of characters I grow to love. Give her books a try if you haven't already!

~ JoAnne W.

"To walk through the door of unlimited possibility, we have to leave behind our fears, our self-doubt, and our persistent disbelief. We have to leave behind our pain and suffering; our resentment. Our frustration. Our impatience. We have to leave behind the story we tell about our past. This work is about believing in a new story – and learning how to behave as a new person until we become it. About coming into contact with a deeper aspect of ourselves."
~ Dr. Joe Dispenza

1

"Do I have to order you to take time off, Margaret?" Dr Elizabeth Buckley carefully folded her stethoscope and gestured for Maggie to get dressed before returning grimly to her desk. "Make no mistake, it's not a case of if you will suffer a heart attack. It's when you will suffer one."

She briefly thumbed through her medical file while waiting for Maggie to return to her chair. As she sat down before her, she looked up from reading through her medical history and leant toward her. Her green eyes flashed accusingly at her, and her delicate blonde eyebrows burrowed deeply.

"I know you mean well, Liz, but I can't take time off now. All I need is one more month to pull this deal together. So much is at stake. The reality is that if I quit now, I may as well call it a day."

"I wish I could help, Maggie. But, I'm urging you not just as a friend but as your Doctor – your blood pressure is through the roof, your heartbeat is erratic, and you're adrenalised to the max. It's a miracle you haven't collapsed."

"it's true. I've been working hard. But it will return to normal in one month, and I can relax. "

"I don't think you realise how serious this is, Maggie. You seem to be under the illusion that your heart is something you can control. You can think you buy yourself an extra month. Well, Maggie Green, I've got news for you. You can endure more stress than the average person, but even you have limitations."

"What do you suggest I do? Chuck everything I've worked for in and sit under a tree somewhere meditating?" she said crossly.

"Don't be so dramatic. You've been telling yourself that workaholic story all your life. It's time to tell yourself a new story—one with plenty of chapters about rest. Take a break, put your feet up, and go somewhere nice, somewhere you've always wanted to go but could never find the time. You've changed recently. I've noticed it. We all have. Quite frankly, I'm worried about you, Maggie. You've lost your sparkle, your humour. You've lost you. You've become so brittle and short-tempered. I don't mean to be unkind; I'm saying this as your friend."

The words stung, biting into the fragile core of her self-esteem. She hated criticism, but this time the words especially hurt. It was true. Dr Buckley was summing up what she had always feared. She was brittle, hardhearted, uncaring, and unlovable. She fought back tears and slumped back in her chair.

"Do yourself a favour, take time off, recharge, rediscover the Maggie I used to know. The Maggie we all love."

"All right."

"Promise me?"

"Yes, I promise." Maggie got up dejectedly and made her way to the door. She walked out of her office into the cool

Manhattan air. As she merged with the busy pedestrian highway, swimming with New York's most successful elite, the reality of her situation hit with a thud.

She, Maggie Green, Ms Invincible, was burnt out.

Her health was at risk, and other than Dr Elizabeth Buckley, nobody cared. Everything she had worked so hard for suddenly seemed insignificant. The reality was that other than her work, she had nothing.

Nothing and nobody.

It would be alone if she were to go away, as incredible as the notion was.

2

Maggie had heard Venice was beautiful, but nothing prepared her for the flood of emotions that overwhelmed her as she stepped from the train station and saw the Grand Canal for the first time three days after leaving New York.

It was such a relief to arrive safely, and as she took in the magical, heart-wrenching view, a lifetime of stress melted away. The beauty of Venice struck her as soon as she arrived, and the symphony of sounds that permeated the air instantly transported her to a past where life was simple, and beauty was revered. It was so unlike New York, where she felt that the modern, not the antique, was glorified. Where she felt only as good as her last deal.

She heaved a great sigh of relief, grateful to have left her life momentarily behind. One month would go quickly enough in most places, but it would seem like a lifetime here.

"We should be able to see this place in a few hours," she overheard a man say to his wife. "There's nothing but a few churches and a lot of water."

She looked at the couple with pity. She felt sorry for their ignorance about all the sights to be seen, the exotic places to go, and the inspirational art to experience first-hand. Maggie, as always, had been thorough in her research—and with good reason. It had been years since she had pursued her life-long interest in art history. Not since—

She quickly changed her thoughts. She didn't want to think about him. She didn't want to revisit memories that only triggered trauma. All she knew was that her dreams had become whims, fantasies only the idle or extraordinarily wealthy could indulge.

Hard work was the road to salvation, she silently affirmed. Her mother had drummed that into her. Maggie Green knew what it was to work hard and sacrifice her needs. For years she had faithfully played the dutiful daughter, boss, sister, and doormat to the masses.

But not now. Not now that she was on a forced sabbatical. Not now, in this beautiful place, where passions which had long lain dormant were spontaneously set free. Not now that her deepest longings soared high above worldly concerns like doves set free against a peaceful blue sky.

Maggie felt invigorated and ready for new adventures. But she would keep her feet firmly on the ground, she reminded herself, averting her gaze to avoid the amorous glances of a far-too-cliched, far-too-handsome Italian man.

Maggie had been warned to be wary of Italian stallions who looked like modern-day cupids, with masses of shiny black curls and boyish faces.

"Watch out for the ones who ask you if you're an artist," her long-time friend and motivational life coach, Chanel, had warned her. "Like a love-starved fool, I fell for their charms, hook, line and lead pencil. Before I knew it, I was being led through twisting narrow streets to what they promised was their own artist's gallery, only to be pinned to the wall in a passionate declaration of love."

Maggie had at first been horrified and then confused.

Chanel had giggled and added, "Actually, it was all rather exciting! I just adored him. He was like my very own Michelangelo, and let's be honest—New Yorkers aren't the most passionate men. A woman needs what a woman needs—and what you need, Maggie is a really good bonk. It would do you a world of good. Let your hair down, lighten up a little, and make wild passionate love a lot!"

"Thanks for the tip, Chanel. I'll try and remember that," Maggie had said politely, her jaw clenching and chills running down her spine. The idea of a romantic liaison, especially with a foreign man, left her cold. She had her reasons, good reasons, and ones she didn't intend to share.

Not with anyone. Thank God she had got rid of the evidence.

3

———

A violent tug on the sleeve of Maggie's dress startled her. She turned around angrily, cross at the intrusion and furious that someone should roughly finger the new black velvet Dolce and Gabbana dress she had purchased for her first trip to Venice.

She flicked back her hair, allowing the heavy curtain of blonde locks to cascade down her back until they settled upon her shoulder blades. Her green eyes narrowed wildly, and her lips pursed crossly. Maggie Green was a formidable opponent and someone not to be messed with.

Her face softened as she looked down at the young girl standing before her.

"*Scusi, Senora*, please help me," the girl pleaded, forcing a bunch of perfectly shaped red roses toward Maggie.

Maggie stepped back suddenly to avoid being scratched by the stiff, long-stemmed blooms and turned to walk away.

The girl with roses followed. She overtook Maggie and looked up at her with pleading eyes, the colour and sheen of melting chocolate. "Only three euros."

Her dull, dark hair sprung around her pale, gaunt face in

mottled curls. Huge, round eyes with the longest lashes Maggie had ever seen peered past her carefully fortified barrier and burrowed into Maggie's soul.

She could have been just another girl begging for money if not for her bulging stomach and the small bundle she carried in her arms. Maggie felt unusually sympathetic toward her.

She wondered how old this girl was and roughly guessed her age to be 14. Too young, Maggie thought sadly, to be raising a child.

She knew her situation intimately. She was not much older when her father had walked out on her mother, leaving behind her and her five younger siblings.

Maggie's childhood ended abruptly as her mother sunk into depression and sought comfort from the icy cold waters of Gordon's gin and the warm bloody lakes of cardboard merlot.

It seemed a matter of course that Maggie, as the oldest, should take over raising her younger brothers and sisters. Only Maggie's fiery nature and dogged determination helped her endure the long hours that working by day and studying by night involved.

A lot of water had passed over the road, and now 25 years later, Maggie was a qualified corporate lawyer and managing director of a large international consultancy firm. Looking down at the scruffy girl beside her, she doubted that life would work out so well for her.

The young woman persevered, pushing the bunch of red roses toward Maggie again. "For my family," she said, gesturing to the bundle in her arms and rubbing a hand on her stomach.

Maggie admired the girl's persistence and wish to provide for her family. Perhaps she wouldn't have believed the girl if she had been in New York. But in Venice, everything took on a rosy glow, and even she, renowned by others as hard-hearted and guarded, felt unusually trusting. Venice was too powerful a seductress, its beauty and mystique too evocative.

Intoxicated by the gilded gondola traversing the Grand Canal, the beauty of the palazzos and churches hugging its shores, and the dancing light that illuminated all the surfaces it touched, Maggie opened her heart.

As she placed her suitcases on the cobbled street, she wondered what difference giving twenty Euros to the young pregnant girl would make. She knew it was far more than the roses were worth. Instead, she decided it would be good to be extra generous and settled on 50 Euros, the equivalent of 100 USD.

As she unclasped her Chanel handbag, the young girl threw the bundle she had held at Maggie. Maggie reached out instinctively to catch it. As the bundle, which Maggie thought was the girl's baby, flew through the air, she snatched Maggie's purse from her hands.

Three roughly dressed men with oily black hair suddenly appeared from the depths of the crowd.

One of them pushed Maggie forcibly to one side. Another roughly swept her suitcases from the pavement and ran at high speed away from her, snaking their way through the bulging crowd.

It happened so quickly that she didn't have time to react. She struggled to regain her balance, powerless to do anything. She wanted to run after them. A man's hand, firmly placed on her shoulder, stopped her in her tracks. A shiver went down her spine.

"Do not move!" A well-educated, Italian voice said in perfect English. "Wait. It is too dangerous."

Maggie momentarily glimpsed a tall, muscular, well-dressed man running toward the thieves.

"*Arrestili! Arrestili!* Stop them!" He called urgently in English and Italian as he pushed through the crowd.

A wave of pain surged through Maggie. She clutched her chest. "I can't...can't...can't breathe," she gasped, her face contorting as her lungs constricted.

She was barely aware of the crowd of concerned people drawing closer as her eyes flickered and she drifted in and out of consciousness. Her head felt dizzy. Her legs felt numb. Her heart felt dead. She struggled to maintain her balance. Unable to fight losing consciousness, she surrendered to the darkness that descended like a heavy velvet curtain.

A splash of water suddenly brought her back to life. She awoke to find the tall, dark, arrestingly handsome stranger's concerned face staring down at her. She temporarily lost herself in the depths of his hazel eyes and the sensuality of his full, plump lips. They could have belonged to any one of the thousands of cupids that adorned churches throughout Venice, she mused dreamily.

4

SHE WAS A BEAUTIFUL WOMAN MAURO
TOFFOLA THOUGHT TO HIMSELF,
CAPTIVATED BY THE SHIMMERING WAVE OF
GLOSSY BLONDE HAIR THAT SWUNG OVER
HER CHEST AS SHE SAT UP. HER SKIN WAS
THE COLOUR OF THE FINEST PORCELAIN
CHINA, AND HER EYES WERE A BRILLIANT
GREEN, LIKE THE EMERALD LAGOONS
SURROUNDING VENICE.

She was a beautiful woman Mauro Toffola thought to himself, captivated by the shimmering wave of glossy blonde hair that swung over her chest as she sat up. Her skin was the colour of the finest porcelain china, and her eyes were a brilliant green, like the emerald lagoons surrounding Venice.

"Will you be alright?" he said gruffly, his expression changing from concern to a cultivated blend of indifference and disdain.

"I feel dizzy," Maggie said, falling back upon the ground. Mauro rushed to cushion her fall. Maggie tried again to rise slowly to her feet. He held his hand out and allowed her to use his strength.

She stumbled slightly and leaned against him to brace herself. His body softened as though instinctively wanting to merge with hers, then stiffened as he fought against an urge he'd vowed never to feel.

"What happened? I don't remember anything. Only that I was falling. Then everything went black. Where am I?"

"You were tricked by some gypsies. I ran after them, but they escaped down like water rats in the labyrinth of narrow alleys."

"My suitcases? My money?" Panic rose in her voice as she searched for her belongings. She felt disoriented. "I feel so ..." her voice trailed as she tottered dangerously on her impractical heels. She leant against him to steady herself again.

Mauro searched the crowd looking for the man who would claim her. Such a beautiful woman would not be alone. But he saw no one. Offering his body as a crutch, he put his arm around her and held her tightly against his powerful chest. "Signora, where is your husband?"

"My husband? There is no husband. Why would there be?" she said crossly.

Mauro briefly looked down at the gold band she wore on her wedding finger.

"No one?" he questioned.

"No one," she said. Then aware of him looking again at her ring, she added, "I thought if I wore a wedding ring I would be safe."

"Safe?"

"You know from—" Men who preyed on women travelling alone, she wanted to say.

Sensing his confusion, she tried to distance herself from him.

"I am sorry to have been so much trouble. Thank you for helping me. I am grateful. I will be all right now, " she said wearily. Then, suddenly overwhelmed by everything, she burst into a flood of tears. What the hell was wrong with her.

She was Iron Woman. She never cried. Not since—she pushed the unwelcome memories aside.

"I want to go home," she said, raking her fingers through her hair as she dissolved into a cascade of tears.

"I never wanted to come here at all. My doctor made me. How ironic is that? Just my luck to get mugged only minutes after arriving," she said, aware she was babbling.

Her tears made Mauro feel very uncomfortable. He shifted edgily on his feet. Anger, not at her, but toward the villains who had caused her such distress, raced through his veins.

"Why do you think marriage will make you safe?"

She shrugged. "I thought—"

"No, you didn't think. You were foolish. Do you not know anything?" He said, more gruffly than he intended. Why did he care? he wondered, suddenly alarmed at the unwelcome feelings the beautiful damsel in distress was eliciting.

"The gypsies are the vermin of Venice, running like rats at night, preying on anything and anyone to fill their stomachs. They are worse than the plague. The city is full of them. Just like the city is full of tourists like you. Why do you people keep coming here? You complain about the heat, complain about the crowds, complain about the stench," he said briskly.

"I want to go home," she sobbed.

"Go home. It sounds like a sensible idea," he said, looking around the crowd as though planning his escape route home. He was doing a pretty good job at faking hostility. He hated himself for his rudeness. It wasn't her fault he had sworn to stay away from beautiful women. He had made a promise. His word, once given, was never broken.

"But for the moment, you, we," he corrected, "must be practical." You have no money, no passport, nothing. You are distressed. You cannot stay here in this condition. Come with me. I will see what I can do to help."

"With you? Where?" Her emerald eyes regarded him warily.

"Tomorrow, you can go to the police. But it will not matter; they can do nothing about these terrible people. But at least you can ask the police to help you. Perhaps they will have connections with your embassy. Are you American?" he asked.

"Yes," she said. "New York is my home."

"Tonight, my home is your home. We will take the Vaporetto to San Marco to spare you from walking," he said briskly, leading her by the elbow through the busy Venetian streets.

Where was he taking her? And where would this lead?

5

Leaning on him for support, she allowed herself to be led as they boarded one of Venice's many water taxis.

Her worries temporarily left her as the Vaporetto wove its way down the Grand Canal, passing by some of the most majestic architectures, palaces and churches she had until now only seen in magazines and her favourite movies.

At the Vaporetto stop for Piazza San Marco, the tall, dark stranger signalled to her that it was time to disembark. Like a ruler commanding his people, he sliced his hand through the air, gesturing to the crowds trying to embark and disembark to clear a space for Maggie to follow.

She followed quickly, not wanting to lose sight of this man who, for this moment, was her only security, the only hope she had of finding shelter for the night.

She had never felt so vulnerable. All her life, she had fought hard to be in control, to never find herself in a situation where she would have to rely on anyone else for her survival. That had been her mother's mistake. One Maggie vowed she would never allow herself to make.

She felt guilty about not being more appreciative of the

stranger's help. But Maggie felt resentful that her vacation had begun so stressfully. She felt anger rise in her chest. It was the best that she could do not to feel despair at finding herself at his mercy.

As she trailed behind him, she sensed her feelings of obligation were mutual. He was polite but cool and indifferent toward her. He was endeavouring to do enough to be considerate but careful not to overstep the mark. She respected that. But at the same time, she felt obliged to him somehow. As though she was an unwelcome intruder in his life that he couldn't wait to offload.

Even though she felt weak, she decided she wouldn't give him the satisfaction of making her feel indebted to him or of him feeling superior. Besides, it had irked her considerably when she recollected how his body had stiffened and pulled away as she fell against him, as though she was some diseased person he found distasteful in some way.

She guessed from his elegant clothes and impeccable manners that his upbringing prevented him from rejecting her and leaving her to fend for herself, as her patriot New Yorkers would do. She recalled a Candid Camera segment once showing a woman falling down some steps, and despite the obvious pain she suffered and the fact that she did not rise again, nobody, not a soul, went to her assistance. Instead, New Yorkers glanced in her direction and glanced away, perhaps in some vain effort to pretend they had not noticed her at all.

But here in Venice, it was different. Not only had this stranger come to her aid, but he was offering her a bed for the night.

The horror of the situation suddenly struck her. She realised she knew nothing about him and of his true intent. Hell, she didn't even know his name. What was she thinking?

For all she knew, he could be part of the gypsies plot and was leading a poor dazed, and guileless woman to her ruin.

As he strode ahead, she slowed her pace and looked around her to see where she could take refuge.

"What are you doing?" his dark brows knitted into an annoyed frown as he turned around. He clasped her by the elbow and led her through the crowds. "Come quickly."

What was his hurry? And where was he taking her?

6

She felt a run of adrenalin surge inside her as the few pockets of energy reserved for times of danger heightened her senses. The stranger led her through a maze of backstreets lined with apartments three stories high and plastered in an array of dazzling terracottas, lemony yellows, soft pinks and sky blues.

Ordinarily, she would have lingered to touch the walls, allowing the history and the stories these buildings could tell to permeate through her fingers, feeding her mind with an array of imaginings. But today was no ordinary day, and she was not a woman in control of her time.

Maggie took only the slightest comfort in the knowledge it was the height of the tourist season, and many people could come to her rescue should something happen to her.

They walked briskly through Piazza San Marco past the vendors that sold tacky postcards and scentless roses. The streets closest to the Piazza were full of expensive tasteless items purchased by oddly dressed tourists who poured over Venice in their masses with their thick white walking socks and Velcro clasping sandals.

Beyond the Piazza, the dark alleyways still made her nervous, and she soon became disorientated. She had reasoned that as long as she could see the golden archangel Gabriel perched on top of Campanile di San Marco, she would always be able to find her way back to the safety of other tourists.

But here, in the depths of this architectural maze, she had long lost sight of any homing reference. She had only her intuition and the trust in a man she barely knew to save her.

Sensing her disquiet, he turned suddenly.

"Don't worry, I'm not going to kill you."

His words only served to unnerve her even further. Why would he say such a thing, she worried as they stepped deeper and deeper into the labyrinth.

He took a sharp left turn and suddenly stopped.

"We are here."

7

———

Maggie stood in front of the doorway she could only describe as unassuming. Glancing around her, she felt reassured that it looked like any other apartment building and blended in with its surroundings. She expected the interior to be similar.

As Mauro inserted a large brass key into the lock and turned it slowly, Maggie expected to be greeted by a sterile apartment devoid of any personality, just like its owner. It seemed clear to her that he lacked any emotion, so she thought it highly unlikely that he would furnish the apartment with any flair, warmth or passion.

Nothing could have prepared her for what lay inside.

The door swung open, revealing fresco-lined walls surrounding a huge light-filled foyer, which opened to the sky. In the centre was a marble fountain of bubbling water surrounded by cupids. To the left was a wrought iron spiral staircase, which followed a gracefully curving set of marble stairs circling up four levels.

It was a palace!

No, not just any palace, she mused as she registered the

original Venetian floors, antique sculptures and ancient frescos. It was literally a work of art.

As she walked toward the fountain, the beauty of the frescos and artworks that adorned the plastered walls assailed her senses. For a moment, she felt as though she had escaped her fate and escaped into a world of beauty and enchantment.

"My mother lives in that apartment," he said, pointing to the door straight ahead. "She is frail and alone, like you. I look after her."

She suppressed a protest as she followed behind him. She, Maggie Green, was not a frail woman. Ordinarily, she was fierce, formidable and fearless. Today she was just in awe.

He guided her to the first floor. "This is the guest apartment. It will be your place of rest for the night. It has everything you need. If you need me, I will be up there," he said, pointing to the third and fourth floors. "But now I must go and care for my mother."

He produced his set of keys and opened the door to her apartment, revealing a simple entrance room full of antiques, paintings and a small intricately carved hall table, chair and a stand for umbrellas. "I hope you will be comfortable. I will leave in the morning for golf. You can let yourself out. Please leave the key where you found it," he said, pointing to a vessel on the antique table. "Now, please excuse me."

Maggie stood, her mouth wide open, as he disappeared down the stairs to his mother's apartment and closed the door behind him.

She thought New Yorkers were rude, but despite his kindness in coming to her aid, he must be the most disrespectful man she had ever met.

Not only had he not taken the trouble to show her around her apartment, to make sure she was familiar with where to find everything, but he made no attempt to help her find the necessary people to report her theft to or help her find The United States Consulate.

She was left with the very real feeling that he felt that having delivered her to the safety of his palace, he was free of any further obligation to her.

Still, he obviously had concern for his mother, and she was grateful for the kindness he had shown her. Tired from the day's events, she couldn't wait to shower and relax.

8

----

aggie's heart skipped a beat, and her eyes danced joyfully as she stood back and surveyed the surroundings. The apartment was long and wide. The high ceilings and windows lining the south wall filled the room with natural light, giving it a more spacious feeling.

She walked quickly through the space, taking in all the rooms. To the right, a large lounge led to a patio with a little balcony looking out onto the Grand Canal. Geraniums and other brightly coloured flowers perfumed the air and spilt over the edge of the wrought iron railings.

She stood on the small terrace and surveyed the rooftops of the other Venetian apartments. In the reflection on the water, she could make out The Campanile and smiled as the bell tolled eight times. Eight had always been her lucky number.

She felt like Lucy Honeychurch in Room With a View, only she was in Venice, not Florence. And she didn't have anyone to mind her. She certainly couldn't count on the stranger.

Despite her worries, the beauty intoxicated her, and she giggled for the first time in years. It was as though some magical elixir had stripped away years of sobriety and solemness, leaving a childish glee and sense of excitement in their place.

She felt a sense of wonderment and mystery as she took in the breathtaking view. Venice was multi-faceted, full of history, and thousand-year-old roof tiles, flaking plaster walls, glinting church spires, street vendors and a rainbow of wooden shutters framing daily Venetian life.

Surrounded by all this beauty and history, it seemed incredibly insignificant for a moment that she had been robbed of all her worldly possessions. Or rather those she had bundled into her suitcase and carried across the Atlantic.

It suddenly struck her how tired she was of being so soberly serious about life, how bored she was of always being the one everyone turned to in a crisis. Now she was experiencing her own predicament. And a prince had come to her rescue. It seemed as ironic as it did magical. If she was honest, it was about time fortune cut her a break.

For years now, she'd been the caregiver. First, it was to her mother and siblings. Then more recently, the hundreds of clients whose affairs she managed. And all the employees who looked to her expectantly for their salary check each month, like baby starlings, their mouths wide open, waiting for food to be brought to them. It always seemed such a thankless task.

Nobody stopped to think how much effort was required to run a successful international law practice. The demands never let up. The hours she worked were never enough. The TV dinners she quickly ate were empty of nourishment, echoing the emptiness of her life.

I can't believe I've given my life to work, she thought sadly as she surveyed the view again. What would my life have been like if I had come sooner?

Perhaps Dr Elizabeth Buckley had been right. She needed to create a new story for her life. She needed to find herself. Her true self. Now, free of her life's responsibilities, she might write a new chapter. Or she could tell a new story about the future she wanted to experience and reinvent herself completely.

It was strange how at home she felt in the stranger's luxurious palazzo, she thought, turning back into the main salon. Her heart leapt for joy as she spied a collection of antique books. She ran her fingers along the spines, reading aloud the names of the various artists, Titan, Carpaccio, Veronese, Giorgione…names of artists she had studied years ago at school. There was even a book about the British artist JW Turner who had travelled to Venice and loved it so much he created a new body of work.

Seeing the names of art-world titans reawakened dormant passions buried under piles of precedents, legal writs and torts. She couldn't believe her luck to have found herself in such a treasure chest of antiquity and artistic delight.

Her mind turned briefly to the stranger who had led her here. She knew nothing of him, not even his name. Perhaps she had been wrong to write him off as cold and distant. Surely no man who collected and surrounded himself with so much beauty could be hard at heart, she thought as she sat down on the velvet chaise lounge and ran her finger over the ornately carved antique mahogany arms.

Dr Buckley was right. She had tied her identity to the stories she'd forced upon herself. There would be so much freedom in releasing her workaholic, fierce-lawyer report and surrendering to the unknown. She told herself it wouldn't feel so scary if she looked at it like an adventure. Besides, her time in Venice might be the only opportunity to gain some pleasure in her life. Instead of feeling like a victim, Maggie decided to make the most of it.

9

"You're late," Lucia Toffola scolded as Mauro entered her apartment.

"Mamma," Mauro said, kissing her cheek, "I came as soon as possible."

"Where were you?"

Mauro hesitated. He only had to mention he had spent time with another woman, and his mother would be distraught. He couldn't say a beautiful blonde with mesmerising green eyes had fallen into his arms. He couldn't admit how his breath caught, and his heart raced when she fell against his chest. He could not, would not, confide that an American femme fatale now lay under his roof, about to slip into his bed.

Not his own bed, he corrected, noticing the kick of disappointment in his loins. It would make no difference where Maggie Green slept. His mother was old-fashioned. She lived and yearned for the past. She fought change. Now through the sheer force of her personality, she had decided his future. And Mauro, her dutiful son who did not want to disappoint, had made a promise.

"Where is Marina?" Lucia asked, glancing past his shoulder towards the door.

"I told you," he said gently. She was nearing 80 and had suddenly become frailer. Her memory ebbed and flowed like the waters which threatened to engulf Venice. "Marina went to Dubai."

His mother looked horrified. "Dubai? Why?"

"Because she –" Mauro paused. He had told his mother all this before, but she had either forgotten or refused to remember. He shifted restlessly. Must he do this over again? He was terrified she might suddenly fly at him and make a terrible scene. He wanted to say Marina hates Venice. The weight of tradition suffocates her. She yearns to be free. Instead, he said, "She is visiting friends."

Wasn't that what she had texted him when she left without a word, forcing down the knowledge they both denied.

Dubai, known for its luxury shopping, ultramodern architecture and lively nightlife, ideally suited Marina and her thirst for decadence. He couldn't blame her for not wanting to return to Venice. Dubai was progressive, while Venice clung to the past. Dubai relished the new, and Venice delighted in the old. Dubai valued innovation, and Venice revered its history. Dubai and Venice were like Marina and Mauro— worlds apart.

"Opposites attract," his mother said as though reading his mind.

"Not always," he ventured. "Oil repels water. Day destroys night. War battles with peace."

He wanted harmony, not conflict. He wanted ease, not struggle. He wanted agreements, not confrontation. His mother studied him with shrewd assessment.

"The promise?" His mother's question was less an

enquiry and more a demand. Had she forgotten it had been over eight months since Marina was last seen in Venice?

"I remember." He wished his memory would fail him and provide the perfect excuse to forgo the duty he felt.

How could he? Marina's family were among Venice's founders in the 8th century, as was his. Historians traced the lineage as far back as Roman times. Seeing his mother as the insensitive, severely critical, tyrannical matriarch would be easy.

But she had her reasons, and Mauro tried to sympathise with his mother's past. She was a woman of experience and worked hard to gain respectability. She understood Venetian society's intricate workings in which the ruling families' interest was supreme. She was also very much aware of her only son's unique place in society. And Lucia Toffola knew what a formidable union Mauro and Marina would forge. What she couldn't concede was that no love existed between them.

His mother had always been a relatively remote figure in his life. She was not especially warm. He reminded himself that her stiff manner was shared amongst the old-fashioned patriarchal ladies who clung to tradition. Nevertheless, she was forceful.

Mauro glanced at the self-portrait his father had painted in oil months before his death. He had felt closer to his father – a sensitive, kind-hearted man he could always confide in. His father had been known for his strength of character as much as he was for his artistic sensibility. He was a gentle, virtuous man weakened by heartbreak. Was Mauro about to make the same mistake?

It was better Marina stayed away. In time they would learn to compromise. They had both made a promise. They both wanted their parents to be happy. They both – he paused.

He was tired of thinking about his future. Their future. His thoughts curled along the marble stairs to the first-floor apartment and arced toward the beautiful woman in his bed.

Dare he heed the whisper of his heart and admit that the present was more compelling? He wanted to focus on today and look forward to a new future. But could he let go of the past?

Silent longings clashed against insistent noise. You made a promise. The desire to be alone conflicted with the desire to be with her. Some things couldn't be reconciled, he mused as he kissed his mother goodbye.

He strolled up the stairs toward the apartment where Maggie Green was alone. Frescos are the most beautiful and enduring of all the arts, he mused as he traced his fingers along the paintings embedded in the plaster walls. The colours purple and yellow were opposites on the colour wheel, as were blue and orange. People say they clash, he mused, studying the image of lovers entwined in a symphony of contrasting colours. But, when their values are aligned, they create a great scheme. A beautiful fresco feeds the hearts and souls of those fortunate enough to abide under their splendour.

Mauro lingered at the entrance to Maggie's apartment. His hand caressed the antique gold door handle. His mind caressed her thighs. His body rose in urgent need. There would be, could be, no rapture tonight, he vowed, forcing his hand away.

His destiny was decided. In the morning, she would leave. Maggie and his mother would never meet, and no one would be the wiser.

10

―――――

Maggie fell exhausted into bed but struggled to sleep. She kept thinking of work and all the clients and staff she was responsible for. And then she worried about how she would replace her passport, phone, and all the other things she had lost. But mostly, she felt guilty. Guilty for walking away from all her responsibilities. Guilty for putting her needs first. Guilty for placing herself in such a vulnerable position.

Maggie's doctor had told her that even the busiest people must make time for themselves. It seemed ironic that she had to travel so far in search of time-out. But it would only be fleeting, she thought sadly, recalling the heavy workload awaiting her when she returned.

She couldn't pinpoint when she lost her passion, and life became a series of 'have to's and 'must have's'. She couldn't remember the point at which she traded the longings of her heart. She couldn't think of the moment the stirrings of her soul were traded for a chequebook that balanced and material goods to be consumed and retirement planning for a secure future.

Every penny she earned was poured into her business and other ventures that promised a healthy return and paid her staff's wages. Perhaps one day all her sacrifice and all those relentless hours might all pay off, she thought wearily, as she closed her eyes and snuggled amongst the luxurious Italian cotton sheets.

As she drifted off to sleep, the stranger appeared in her dreams. He looked intensely at her as though he could see through her soul, undressing her with his alluring hazel eyes. She smiled as he gathered her into his arms and drew her face to his lips.

"Kiss me, kiss me," she pleaded in her dream as his mouth teased hers, circling her lips with his strong probing tongue.

She was too weak to resist, too smitten to protest, and soon fell into a deep sleep, surrendering entirely to the fantasy.

* * *

SHE OPENED her eyes in fright, suddenly aware of a dark shadowy figure standing at the foot of her bed. Instinctively she reached out for the Venetian glass lamp beside her bed and switched it on.

"*Susci*, it is only me. Mauro."

She sat up in bed and drew the sheets up around her naked body. "How dare you come into my room like that. Frightening me in this way. I was asleep. You nearly gave me a heart attack."

She had not heard the key turn in the lock, nor Mauro

enter the room. It alarmed her that he should still have a key, but secretly she felt relieved that it was only him.

"Are you alright? I heard you cry out," he said.

Maggie blushed, suddenly remembering her dream. Had he heard her beg him to kiss her?

"I'm sorry. I did not mean to scare you. I only wanted to make you comfortable and to see if you were safe," he said, holding an oversized white cotton man's shirt out toward her.

She wanted to tell him that she always slept naked but decided it was none of his business, and besides, she didn't want to encourage him in any way.

He was staring at her strangely, and she looked with horror to see that the sheet had fallen away, exposing her right breast. Although the air was hot and humid, her nipple was erect and pertly, claiming his attention.

She pulled the sheet firmly up around her and reached out, abruptly removing the shirt from his hands.

He smiled briefly before quickly regaining his composure.

"You must be tired. I am pleased to see that you are well. I will check with you in the morning, and we will make arrangements together. I have golf, as I said, but after, I will return. Please wait for me. *Buona notte*," he said, bowing his head and quickly exiting the room.

Mortified, Maggie pulled the sheets over her head. I can't believe I sat there talking with him with my right breast exposed. If I wasn't highly embarrassed, it would almost be laughable, she thought, lifting the sheets and reaching for the shirt he had left. After pulling his shirt over her head, she got up and went to the door to check that it was locked securely.

She got back into her bed, exhausted and humiliated and tossed and turned for several hours before drifting into a restless sleep.

11

Voices outside her window the following morning startled Maggie and woke her from her dreams. *"Permissio! Permissio!"* cried the various voices of street vendors struggling to make their way through the crowds of tourists who wove their way through the narrow streets below.

She glanced around the bedroom and was momentarily started by the lack of familiarity. Original works of art adorned her bedroom walls, depicting scenes of historic Venice.

The beauty of the oil paintings had not diminished over time. Scenes of gondolas tethered to posts outside The Doges Palace and The Grand Canal filled with various sea-fearing vessels. Many of them were merchant ships, depicting the days when Venice was at its height as the merchant capital of the world.

The scenes filled Maggie with wonder, and she stretched out lazily in the four-poster bed. The luxurious feeling of the Italian cotton sheets did not miss her attention. She knew an excellent quality sheet when she felt it. The cotton was soft, and the cream and gold quilted bed cover made her feel like a princess.

Beside her, a crystal tumbler and pitcher of water had been thoughtfully left for her. It sat upon an antique bedside table beside a Venetian glass lamp which gently diffused the room with rosy pink light.

She looked at the window where the sun tried to force its way through the heavily shuttered windows. She got up from her bed and glimpsed briefly at herself in the vast ornate gilded mirror, which hung from the wall opposite her bed, before walking to the window and pushing back the bright green painted shutters to reveal the streets below.

Only meters away, she had a clear view of the palazzo opposite her, where a beautiful Italian woman with black silky hair passionately embraced her husband.

Even though Maggie knew it was impolite to look, she could not take her eyes off them and secretly wished it was her. It had been years since she had allowed a man to hold her. Years since she had felt the warm flood of desire surge through her body, bringing a warm glow to her face and eyes.

Life in New York, she thought sadly, was hard and grey like old concrete, rough to the touch and devoid of sensuality. To survive, she had cut off her feelings and denied her femininity. Life as a corporate lawyer was brutal and cutthroat. Only the tough survived, especially in the board rooms of Manhattan. It was no wonder she felt burnt out, dried up and discarded.

She turned and stood before the mirror and looked at herself earnestly. On the surface, she probably looked like she had it all. Long legs to kill for and long flowing locks the colour of gold that never failed to draw a stare. Men desired her. She knew that, but she always kept them at arm's length. They only brought trouble and distracted her from her career.

Distractions could be fatal, she reminded herself, resulting in mistakes that cost time and millions of dollars in lost revenue. Her thoughts turned to the dark, handsome stranger who had reluctantly come to her aid. She felt strangely drawn to him. Who wouldn't? She smiled as she recalled how he had led her through the streets of Venice and settled her in his palace.

Tall, dark and handsome. He held the promise of a cliched romantic liaison. She resolved that it was one she would not be pursuing, drawing the shirt he had left for her tightly around her chest.

The scent of his cologne made her feel slightly dizzy, and she noticed with curiosity the strange way her body tingled. She swept aside the erotic thoughts that sprung to her mind, uninvited and unwanted.

A knock on the door startled her. Who could that be?

"I'm surprised you didn't just barge in. I thought you had a key," she said, carefully replacing the trill of joy she truly felt with a terse detached tone.

She surveyed Mauro as he stood in the doorway. He looked even more handsome than she remembered. He was dressed in a fine Italian wool suit, striped shirt, lemon cashmere vest, and baby pink bow tie. One of many qualities she admired about the Italians was how they always looked impeccable, no matter what they wore.

She glanced at his feet. You could always tell a man by the quality of his shoes. She'd spurned one suitor solely based on his white, velcro clasping shoes. "They're easy to put on," her spurned lover had protested in his defence.

Once again, Mauro didn't disappoint. His beautiful, tan leather shoes glistened with polish and oozed quality that only the finest leather could impart.

She smiled thoughtfully. He was adorable but totally unsuitable, she quickly reminded herself. She hadn't forgotten the humiliation of the previous night or the curt way he had treated her initially. If there was one thing she detested more than Brussels sprouts, it was arrogance and aloofness in a man. That, and feeling vulnerable. Maggie resolved to begin the day in a stronger position. "Do you always make a habit of creeping up on women?" she demanded.

"I did not mean to cause embarrassment," he said.

Maggie thought she saw a smile briefly touch his lips. "Apology accepted," she said quickly, surprised by his conciliatory tone.

As he stepped toward her, she drew her arm across the doorway barring his entry, conscious that her bra and panties lay on the bed. He stiffened and frowned.

"I have come to escort you to the police so that you may have a chance to recover your things. I would have thought you would be dressed by now. It is after 11 am. Do you usually make it a habit to stay so late in your bed?" he said impatiently.

"Perhaps if my sleep hadn't been so rudely interrupted, I might be less tired," she threw back at him. Nobody ever spoke to her like she was a petulant child. Who did he think he was, she thought furiously.

"I see you are easily aroused," he said, smiling softly at her.

"I'm not sure what you find so amusing," she said, drawing her hands to her hips.

"Perhaps, it is because you insist on revealing your breasts to me," he said, looking her up and down and studying her intently.

To her horror, she realised that she had forgotten to button the shirt properly, and as she had unfolded her hands, it draped open, revealing her porcelain white skin and well-rounded breasts. As she stood nearly naked before him, she wished the tiled floor would open up and swallow her. Instinctively she slammed the door shut.

"I will call for you in fifteen minutes. Please be dressed," he said, through the keyhole, laughing softly as he disappeared into his apartment. "We must leave directly, and I would prefer it if you could cover yourself and act with some dignity when we appear in public."

God, I can't believe it. First, the sheet drops and now his shirt flops open, revealing everything, she cringed in dismay. How on earth was she ever going to be able to look at him with a straight face? Perhaps it was just as well that he would help her find the police. Hopefully, they would help her find her belongings. She never wanted to see that smug man again. How dare he tell her how she should act and behave in public. The cheek of that man. He didn't even know her.

And he never would.

13

Mauro called for her precisely 15 minutes later. Maggie usually admired punctuality, but now it only frustrated her. How could she possibly even begin to get ready? She had none of her things, not even a hairbrush.

God, I must look like a mess, she thought dismally, aware that this was the first time in years she had been seen without a full set of make-up and her hair immaculately groomed.

She had only had enough time to run her fingers through her blonde tresses. Usually, she would have spent hours fastidiously applying make-up and slowly and repeatedly pulling the heated irons she had found in the bathroom through her unruly curls until beaten into submission, they fell into straight and smooth locks down her back. She had always hated her Nicole Kidman ringlets that sprung like coils from her head.

"Do you have everything you came with? We shall not be returning," Mauro said matter of factly as she appeared from the bathroom. How beautiful she looks, he thought to himself, like the model from Botticelli's Renaissance masterpiece, The Birth of Venus. Mauro savoured her pale skin and unadorned face and recalled how he loved natural beauty in a woman. He never knew why women insisted on plastering a riotous palette of colour on their faces and masking their true radiance.

Her near-nakedness excited him more than he dared realise. The power she had over him both alarmed and intrigued him. It was so uncharacteristic of him. He was usually so reserved, so dutiful, so cautious. He drew a deep breath and steadied himself. No good ever comes of hot-blooded passion, he reminded himself. Hadn't his mother instilled that in him when she convinced him to make his promise?

The promise!

He shook his head, trying to dislodge the commitment that lay in the rapidly approaching future.

"Follow me," Mauro said sombrely, walking quickly out of the apartment, away from her spell.

Obediently, she followed him down the spiral staircase out onto the busy streets below. He walked quickly ahead of her and then stopped abruptly. "*Permisso*," he said, taking his hand gently and placing it under her elbow. "It is easy to get lost."

Her flesh tingled with longing. Her mind raced, trying to understand rationally her body's secret longings, her heart's true desires.

14

———

He turned toward the Campanile and led her quickly and skilfully through the streets. As they approached Piazza San Marco, his pace slowed, and she noticed a soft, peaceful glow settle upon his face, his tight lips softened, and a small smile settled upon his lips.

Curious to see what had captured his attention, she followed his gaze and was surprised to see that a quintet of musicians were the source of his incredible happiness.

He intrigued her, for his brisk manner and reserved nature seemed so out of character with someone who would love classical music.

"Is that really Florien's café?" Maggie asked him.

"Si, Caffè Florian," he corrected.

"It's so beautiful. It's like in the movies with the pigeons flying in the piazza and all the rich and the famous and not so famous sitting with their backs to the musicians, gazing out at the piazza, sipping the most expensive cappuccinos in the world."

He looked irritated. "Is that all you Americans think about? Coffee and who is famous. Listen instead to the music, the incredible sounds, and the passionate playing. Do you see the first violinist? See how he commands the stage. See how he stands. He is obviously classically trained. You can tell by the way he plays."

His voice tapered off as he stood and listened to the music, deeply entrenched in his thoughts. He closed his eyes momentarily, losing himself in the music of Vivaldi.

She looked at his face earnestly, trying to fathom his true intent. It seemed unlikely that a villain with intentions to decapitate her would be so profoundly moved by the melodic sounds of the violins, accordion and piano, she rationalised.

Long, thick lashes sprung from his closed lids and gently kissed his cheeks. His naturally tanned skin looked smooth and was a shade that bore a delicious resemblance to her favourite caramels. He was classically handsome, she surmised.

He held himself with the surety and confidence of a man who had never known poverty. His palatial home and clothes echoed this fact. His jacket and trousers were made from the finest Italian wool, and his crisp pink striped shirt was made from the finest Italian cotton. A purple and pink spotted bow tie made of silk combined well with the rest of his clothing, conveying an imaginative, artistic aristocratic streak.

The searing mid-afternoon sun bore down on them both and illuminated the natural highlights that intermeshed through his hair and illuminated his soft curls.

He stood at least three heads taller than her, and his posture and stature reassured her that this was a man of some distinction, not a rogue. Still, other than his first name and where he lived, she knew nothing of him, and her curiosity could be silenced no longer.

"Are you a musician?" she asked. "You seem so knowledgeable about music."

For the briefest moment, she thought she detected a wave of deep sadness rise within, forcing a flicker of recollection to move to his eyes.

But Maggie could not be sure because it passed so quickly.

"I am an architect," he said. Offering no further explanation.

"An architect?" she cried with admiration. "Wow! That must be fabulous, especially here in Venice. You are surrounded by the most brilliant architecture. Tell me, what is it like? What are you creating?"

"There is so little room for creativity here," he said sadly. "Everything is protected, and we are only allowed to work on restoration—much time is spent ensuring everything complies with stringent historical rules. I also run an antique gallery," he said, slightly brightening. "It has been in my family for many years. Tradition is critical."

"Don't you yearn to break free now and then? Throw caution to the wind? Live a little?" she asked him, sensing his sadness and a heavy cloud surrounding him.

"How can I expect you to understand?" he said, sighing deeply as he moved into the thronging crowd again. "Please, come. We must find the tourist police."

15

"I am sorry they were not able to be of more help. But it is as I suspected. The Gypsies are too many, and the police too few. I am afraid you will never possess your things again," Mauro said, leading her out of the *Polizia di Stato.*

"It's okay. Honestly, I never thought I'd have much chance of finding my things again," Maggie said. "Besides, they are only possessions, and I have insurance. I need to phone the office and get my secretary to grab my policy number and wire me some money. I'd be very grateful if you would allow me to stay for a few more days."

She hated asking him to help her, being beholden to him in any way, but he was the only hope she had of a bed for the night, and if that meant swallowing her pride, then that was the price she was prepared to pay. Besides, she thought, as she surveyed him, there were worse ways to spend her days—and nights.

A crazy reckless thought entered her mind. Maybe Chanel had been right. What harm would a fling have? History didn't need to repeat. Maggie was older and wiser now. She wasn't the naive 18-year-old who had been seduced, tricked, and almost blackmailed. That was an old story. One she didn't want to relive. She would not be conned again. Once she got her money, she'd be out of there and never have to see Mauro again.

The truth was she needed the physical release. It had been years since she'd had hot, passionate sex with anyone. As long as nobody got hurt, what was the harm? Besides, there was something mysterious about this man, something that couldn't help but excite her.

He'd already seen her pretty much naked, so what was to stop them going all the way? Nothing but her own closed heart and fear of being hurt again, she thought warily, pushing any thoughts of hot passionate sex out of the way. Besides, she reminded herself that he obviously wasn't interested in her, or he would have made a pass already.

****

She's a fiery wee thing, Mauro thought to himself. So different from the crowds of women that he had met before. She was so independent and self-contained. Her elusiveness intoxicated him. Women threw themselves at him every day. Why wouldn't they, he thought. He was tall, dark, classically handsome, extraordinarily wealthy, and one of Venice's most eligible bachelors. His brow crested into a frown. For now, he mused, recalling his promise.

But even though the women that vied for his attention were stunning beauties, they bored him. Like a cat thrown a dead mouse, where is the joy in getting something so readily offered, he reflected. There is none, he mused, smiling to himself.

Mauro was secretly pleased that the police couldn't help Maggie. He liked that she seemed so out of her comfort zone that she was such an unwilling and undemanding woman. She wanted nothing from him, only a place of safety.

A surge of lust coursed through his loins as he recalled the radiant beauty of her breasts. He wanted her. Desired her like no other woman.

"You haven't answered my question? May I stay a while longer?" she asked tentatively.

He frowned, not wanting to give her any sign that the thought excited him.

"It is not so convenient for me," he said, wondering how to keep her hidden from his mother. "I will see what I can do. It will not be easy, but I will do my best," he said. Keeping her from his mother was only a minor factor in his decision not to show too much impulsive recklessness. Mauro decided it was better to show indifference than to let get than to let a woman like her, so clearly used to having her own way, take possession of him.

"I'm not asking to be a kept woman," she said levelly. "I will of course pay. If I may use your telephone, I will arrange for money to be transferred to your account."

"Si. Va bene, of course. You can come directly to my Antique Studio, and we can make arrangements from there. Please come directly at two o'clock. Follow these simple directions," he said, placing his business card in her hands.

His fingers clasped over hers and lingered for a moment longer than necessary. Would it be so wrong, he wondered tentatively, to allow himself the indulgence of a passionate encounter? One last time.

16

―――――――

"Gosh! I have never seen so many treasures in one place," Maggie said as she entered *Galleria d'antiquariato* promptly at two p.m.

Hidden down a dark lane, Mauro's store was an unexpected treasure trove of delight. The walls contained several original Venetian oil paintings, and antique mahogany cabinets housed precious silver trinkets and old Venetian jewellery. Everything oozed passion and intimacy.

"I once went to a psychic woman who said she could foretell my future simply by holding a piece of my jewellery," she said, surprising herself at her revelation. She looked at Mauro, fully expecting him to think she was crazy but instead was caught in his smile.

"And what did this fortune-teller say to you?" he asked.

"It's as if the original wearers of the jewellery and antiques reside here, whispering their stories of love, passion and sexual conquest," Maggie continued, ignoring his question. It sounded so cliched to confide that the psychic had seen a tall, dark stranger in her future. She probably said that to everyone.

Mauro gazed at her in wonderment, amazed and enraptured by her expression. He had never seen a woman react with such emotion. For so long, it seemed he was the only one who cared so dearly for his little antique studio.

Galleria d'antiquariato had been in the family for many generations. Following his father's death when Mauro was only four years old, he eagerly sought the role of continuing the tradition. When he was not consulting and working on architecture projects, and other family commitments, he would retreat there and submerge himself in this treasure trove of antiquity.

He could feel his dearly beloved father's presence every moment he was there. They both shared a secret passion. One his father had gone to his grave with.

His mother always denied the actual cause of his father's premature death, but in his heart, Mauro knew why his father's heart had failed.

His mother knew too, but she kept the truth to herself. Perhaps she was blaming herself in some way. Instead, the record of his death merely registered, unexplained. The secret weighed heavily on him. If only he had somebody he could confide in. Some sign, some encouragement to give him the courage to give life to his father's dormant dreams.

A warm breath upon his cheek made him turn quickly around. Yet no one stood near him. The gold-haired stranger was on the other side of the room, thumbing excitedly through his collection of books on antique Venetian glass.

Mauro shrugged, unable to find the source of the slight breeze surrounding him. He stole a second glance at the beautiful woman who had so quickly entered his life. Her cheeks were flushed, and her eyes danced with excitement.

"Gosh! I can't believe you have so many books about Venetian glass. They're amazing! I do envy you being able to surround yourself with such beautiful things," Maggie said, throwing her arms out wide and spinning carefully around in a tiny circle.

It suddenly struck him that he knew nothing about her. But he sensed she shared a longing, a yearning, a passion for all things visual and beautiful. A strong surge of excitement grew in his stomach, a sense of knowing, of trust. He wasn't yet ready to let her into his heart, but for some strange reason, he felt sure that perhaps this one woman was someone who would not criticise him for his most profound, most heartfelt longings.

Longings that his father shared but had been forced to bury. He wanted desperately to know more about her to test his feelings and certainty for her.

Holding his emotions at bay, he turned to her. "I am so sorry that your visit to Venice has begun so badly," he said earnestly. "I would like to help make your stay easier—and, if you will allow it, more desirable."

The words poured from his mouth before he could contain them. He cursed himself for being so weak. He should distance himself from her. Pay for a hotel. Send her on her way.

Guilt rose from deep within his heart. He felt possessed, unable to hold back the desire that had seized him. His emotions felt like a sea shaken to its core by a tsunami. Desire flooded his groin and impassioned his soul.

"Would you like to meet me for an aperitif this evening?" he asked impulsively.

He was aware he was stepping into dangerous territory. He had to have her. How could he not? He tried, fruitlessly, to bring forth his sense of duty, commitment and promises he made to others. His life, he thought ruefully, was one big series of responsibilities and obligations he carried out dutifully.

Such were the obligations required of an only son. Such were the obligations required of an heir. How could he not honour his mother's desires for her own flesh and blood? How could he break the promise he had made to her?

Family honour and duty weighed on him like a velvet curtain submerged in water, dragging him down, down, down into the dark, cold depths of despair. Stop, he told himself as he studied the beautiful woman with the golden hair that glinted like white, hot fire. What harm would a moment in the sun bring to bear?

None, he thought, hopefully. Perhaps a moment of warmth with her would give him the strength to walk down the path of duty laid for him since time began.

17

Mauro stood waiting earnestly at the entrance as Maggie entered the bar where they had arranged to meet. She loved the way he was so formal and reserved. He has such impeccable manners, she mused as she registered her surroundings. The bar was modern and elegantly laid out. Its streamlined, minimalist interior sharply contradicted the thousand-year-old buildings that dominated Venice.

Soft candlelight gave the room an intimate glow and diffused their awkwardness. They began their evening timidly, both uneasy in each other's company.

Something about him intrigued her. He was a man of plurality, duality, and complexity.

When she was black, he was white. When she was red with anger, he was cool with patience. When she was lost, he was found. He was everything she was not. He looked burdened by some secret he would not reveal, she thought intuitively to herself. Perhaps in this, they were alike. Their hearts' desires were wrapped under layers of protection, distrust and memories too painful to explore.

He sensed her pain. She sensed his unease. Lubricated

and loosened by Bellini cocktails, they gradually opened up to each other, revealing pockets of their history that felt safe to share.

"Why did you become a lawyer?"

"I felt like it would be a way to help people, to bring about change and contribute to our world. I was naive," she said.

A puzzled frown crested his brows.

"I thought I was fighting for justice. I now realise I am fighting for profit. I loved studying law, and I was good at it. But then I started working. That's when things changed. What I experienced didn't match my dreams. There was a strong focus on billing, a very hierarchical system, a focus on profits, and an unhealthy obsession with success. At the same time, relationships and family were sacrificed on the altar of my career. I started measuring my life in 6-minute units. I was promoted and soon made partner. I was offered gold, but I quickly began to realise that the gold was a pair of expensive handcuffs. I thought starting my own business would free me. But the cage only became one of my own making. The system is toxic. Everything is about the dollar. How much can be extracted? How many damages can be awarded? Who can maximise their wins by ensuring their opponents' losses? Finally, the stress took a toll. I'm here on doctor's orders," she confided.

"What will happen when you go back?"

She shrugged.

"Why do you stay in that job?"

"It's all I know."

"What is your passion?"

"My passion?"

"I feel like you want to quit law. You're an intelligent woman. Try something else. Use your desire to help the world in another way. Look into your heart, ask your soul to reveal its greatest desire."

She stared at him, dumbfounded. "My soul?"

"Let go of your head. Lean into your heart."

"Is that why you became an architect?" she asked, wanting to shift off the foreign topic of her heart and hopeful that his answer might reveal something that could show her the way.

"I love beauty. It was that simple. I wanted to create a world where beauty ruled. Like you, architecture has not lived up to my expectations. In part, there are the limitations of working in Venice with so many restrictions. Then there is the constant haggling over money, and crooked contracts, and bureaucratic fools with no eye for beauty and more open to bribes. But mostly, I didn't want to spend my life in front of a screen, doing everything by computer. The modern world—" he paused.

She nodded her agreement. "It seems so ugly against this backdrop of history. That's what I love about being here," she said. "It's like I've travelled back in time. There are no cars, no skyscrapers, just all this history."

"Is that what brought you to Venice?" Mauro asked. "You could have gone anywhere for a rest." He kicked himself for not having something more intelligent to say. For some unexplainable reason, he found it difficult to talk to her. He wanted to convey the warmth he felt in his heart. To reveal his most authentic sentiment, but instead, his words came out like the blocks of ice that floated on the surface of his cocktail. Cool and frigid.

If only she knew how much time he had spent thinking of her since they had first met. Not a single spare moment went by where he was not holding his life up for inspection, reevaluating what he was getting out of his relationships and what he was putting into them.

He felt a wave of loneliness engulf him. Even though he was surrounded by many people, he felt no one really understood him. Until now, he had never met a woman who heard the longings of his soul and held the key to his heart.

Not since Marina, and even then, the feelings she had stirred were nothing in comparison. He had been shocked when she had revealed the truth and extent of her deceit. Perhaps he was foolhardy to even consider trying to make it work. But he had made a promise. They both had. Until then, he was technically free. She was having her last fling, and he…

Mauro realised with a jolt that he felt so dreadfully lonely. He had friends, but no one had ever really got inside of him. Nobody truly felt what he felt. Nobody shared the passion he loved. *Until her.* Mauro felt it was time to radically reappraise his life and the choices he was being forced to make from misplaced loyalty and duty.

Perhaps now was the time to separate himself from the illusions that ran through even the best relationship and to look at what was really there. The answer frightened him. He knew it already. Everything in his life was built on shaky, impermanent foundations which, like Venice, could not withstand the rising waters of his despair.

He stared into his glass. He was becoming despondent. Alcohol always did that. He resolved to stop drinking gin and decisively pushed the glass to one side. It always made him sad. He didn't need alcohol to give him courage, he resolved.

Mauro glanced at Maggie. He was tired of living an empty, passionless life full of duty and tradition. His soul yearned to fly— free to live and to love Maggie.

If that meant a short flight and a crash landing, as long as he protected himself, he felt that perhaps this time, though love would be short, it was a pain he could possibly bear.

Seize the day, he thought. Seize the night.

"Come back to the galleria. It is so magical in the evening," he said impulsively.

18

———

"Please come inside," Mauro said, opening the door. He switched on the lights and dimmed them. As he walked around the studio he lit the candles in the ornate gilded candelabras festooned with cupids that adorned the walls. A rainbow of gentle light permeated the air, softly glowing from the pretty pinks, reds, yellows and blues in the glass of centuries-old Venetian lamps.

Antique cupids suspended from the ceiling silently sang a chorus of ancient love songs and antique lockets whispered the heart-felt longings of ancient suitors. Or so it seemed to Maggie. Her ordinarily sharp, always dubious, sceptical mind had turned to slush, softened by the mellow overtures of the cocktails she had consumed, the antiquities that surrounded her, and the desire that flamed unbidden for the handsome Italian man who had so gallantly come to her rescue.

I wonder what passions lie under that quiet, steady façade, Maggie thought to herself recklessly. Although Mauro kept his cards close to his heart, something about how his eyes floated over her, lingering a moment longer than perhaps even he intended, made her feel confident about his feelings for her.

Then there was the way her spine shivered at even the slightest touch, the tiniest brushes against each other's bodies, the unspoken promises of a caress and deep embraces to come, she mused. I'm so tired of letting the past dictate my future. Fortune favours the bold, she told herself. It's time to create a new story.

Just wait until I tell Chanel, she thought to herself, looking over at him and giggling with delight at the absurdity of her situation. She Maggie Green, who swore never to have an Italian affair, was about to get laid.

"Why do you laugh?" Mauro asked.

"I'm not laughing," Maggie said, smiling. "Not at you anyway. It's just I feel so happy. I haven't felt this happy for a long time. I can't remember the last time I laughed." She reached out her hand and swept it softly down the length of his arm.

Mauro drew her close to his chest. "I feel so happy too. This is unusual for me, but since I first met you, I felt this incredible attraction for you. But my life is so complicated," he stepped back, distancing himself from her.

"What's wrong?" Maggie asked as he pulled away. Have I blown it? Of course, she blamed herself. She always blamed herself. A childhood of shaming had instilled that destructive trait in her psyche.

Mauro strolled to his desk, an old table that ran from one length of the shop to another. It was piled high with a collection of ancient books and drawings.

"No, you have done nothing," he said softly. "Nothing but reveal to me the inevitability of this moment." He stood upon his chair and reached high into the wall-length bookcase that stretched across the studio.

Mauro pulled a book from the shelf, and a large panel opened, revealing a hidden safe. Maggie gasped.

"There is something I must share with you, Maggie. Something I have kept a secret."

19

"I can trust you, Maggie, can't I?" Mauro asked, turning around and staring down at her.

"I'm a lawyer," she said, looking into his eyes and searching his face for any trace of the secret he had yet to reveal. "In my line of work, confidentiality is a given."

"It is as I thought," he said, pulling a small musical case from the hidden panel of the bookcase.

She watched with intrigue as Mauro slowly stepped from the chair onto the floor and stood beside her.

He placed the black case on his desk. It was worn but well cared for. Made from the finest leather, it carried a mellow, slightly luminous soft gloss and smelled of beeswax.

Sentiment settled on Mauro's face and enveloped his body as he gazed at the musical case wistfully. He gently ran his fingers along its length and lifted the lid. Maggie thought she detected a tear welling in his eyes and, aware she was staring at him, turned her face briefly away.

A deep sigh from the depths of his belly brought her gaze back to him.

The combination of the candlelight and the brilliant hue

from the ruby-coloured velvet that lined the case gave his face a rosy glow.

His deep hazel eyes swum with nostalgia and glowed with the look of a man who was deeply in love.

The intensity of his emotions intrigued Maggie, and she felt an invisible thread tugging at her heart, drawing her nearer to him. She stepped forward to be closer to the source of his desire.

"Amore," he said, looking up at her with love as he picked the violin tenderly from its case. "This was my father's," he said gently, running his finger along the top of the sound holes, which curved gracefully towards the centre of the violin. He traced the curve along the bottoms that curved towards the violin's corners.

"Such grace and beauty," he whispered softly. He looked up at her. "Like you," he said tenderly. "Your body is like a violin," he said, slowly raising his finger and tracing her curves in the air. "Soft and rounded, narrow at the neck, fuller here and here," he smiled as his fingertips followed the curve of her breasts, "tight at the waist before blossoming at the hips," he continued before tapering his fingers elegantly once again.

Maggie's body shivered with anticipation as his fingertips hovered centimetres from her. She longed for him to touch her and felt giddy with excitement. She moaned softly, trying to release the passions stirring violently within.

Mauro gently lifted the violin from its case and held it to the light. "This is an exceptional violin, Maggie. Mostly because it belonged to my father, but more than this, it is a Stradivarius. In fact, this is one of the first Stradivarius's ever to have been made."

"A Stradivarius?" Maggie exclaimed. "They are very scarce, aren't they? Very valuable too?"

"Si. This violin is priceless. It is scarce and very sought after. Now there are only eighteen violins known to exist. But more important than its monetary value to my father and myself, it is one of the most beautiful instruments ever made. The music that comes from it is so sweet, pure, and unlike anything you can imagine. It is music, music for my soul."

"I have heard so much about them." Her breath caught in her chest as she spoke, giving a sexy huskiness to her tone. The moment was swoon-worthy. Would Mauro play it for her? Here? Now? In this magical place?

"When my father gave me this violin, I was the happiest boy in the world. See its beautiful golden brown varnish, ah. . .and it's shaped to perfection. My heart leaps every day when I take it out of its case. Its beautiful colour glows. History. Fame. Beauty. Power. 250 years after his death, Stradivari's violins remain the best in the world. No one has ever succeeded in displacing him. No one ever will."

"Do you ever play it?" she asked, hoping wildly but not wishing to ask.

"It carries so many sad memories," he said, running his fingers along the smooth strings. "But now," he turned to her, "I can feel love calling to me."

"Why do you keep it hidden? Surely a treasure like that is to be shared."

Asking a man to share his Stradivari is like asking him to share his wife," he said, smiling. "Should I share you because I find pleasure in you?"

Maggie gulped back a cry of protest.

Mauro placed the violin gently down and stepped toward her. He lifted her face gently to the light, "How beautiful you are," he said, turning her face slightly to view her profile. "Exquisite, priceless, irreplaceable. You are like the rarest of diamonds, the most precious of jewels. I want to drink from your lips to taste the sweetness of your soul."

He pulled her toward him and kissed her. She wilted under his strength and surrendered willingly, drowning in desire. The candles flickered from the few ornate gilded candelabras and the cupids that adorned the walls, then extinguished, leaving only the full moon's soft glow.

A warm breeze encircled them as though somebody lingered close by. His lips still locked upon her, he gently guided her toward the ornate chaise lounge positioned against the back wall and lay her down.

He kissed her neck and slowly worked his way down her body. He sucked on her nipples, pertly rising from her black cocktail dress, and licked at them playfully before sliding the thin straps down with his teeth, exposing her breasts. He cupped them in his hands and, leaning his head down, buried his face in them, inhaling her scent deeply as she moaned with pleasure.

"Don't stop!" She moaned gently, arching her back in ecstasy."Please, don't stop."

"Darling Maggie, I want to give you so much pleasure. Are you ready to experience heaven on earth, my love? To hear the angels sing as only a few have experienced in their whole lives. I want to give you pleasure to make for you this gift that I have never given to another."

He kissed her on the mouth and rose slowly to his feet.

"But first, I want to play for you."

20

S oulful tunes of love danced from the violin. They floated and hovered in the air like the feathers of white doves, riding the soft, warm breezes that filtered through the open window, tickling and delighting her senses. The music moved her unexpectedly, bursting through her chest as though unlocking the key to a chamber that had kept her heart imprisoned for so long.

She didn't want to have a holiday affair with someone she would never see again. Yet something about Mauro drew her toward him.

In the end, she surrendered. Surrendered to his love, so deep and transparent, like the waters of a freshwater lake—pure and untainted.

AFTER THEY MADE LOVE, they lay with their heads side by side, arms around each other, cooing like white doves, happy to have found love in their lives. Emotions swam involuntarily within her. Nameless emotions stirred her heart, forcing tears to appear.

"Why are you crying?" he asked.

"I feel so happy," she said, leaning into his chest. It suddenly occurred to her that she felt peaceful for the first time in her chaotic life. It was as though she had come home. Home to a place of great familiarity and contentment. Home to where her heart was.

He leaned over, kissed her gently, and wrapped his arms around her. His body draped effortlessly over her body.

It seemed so strange now to reflect on how she had shunned him when they had first met. Now, having travelled across the world, she had met a man she adored in the most romantic city in the world, Venice. But soon, reality would suck her back, and the love she felt would be nothing but a dream. She didn't want to think about it now. She only wanted to spend every moment with him.

21

———

They spent the next few days together exploring Venice. She loved his sense of humour. There was something fresh and uncomplicated about him. He possessed an honest, gentle simplicity that she felt drawn to. But he was also strong too. There was a strength that radiated from him. He was Venice's lead architect and a leader in so many other ways too. With him, she felt safe. As they walked the streets of Venice, he wrapped his arms around her and drew her close. For the first time, she felt protected.

She thought it strange that she hadn't met his mother, but Mauro had told her she had gone to visit her sister. Besides, it wasn't as if Maggie was destined to be in Mauro's life for long, so she pushed the niggling thought that Mauro didn't want her to meet his mother aside.

"I remember my passion now," she told him. "As a child, I used to love to draw and paint. I felt so happy. Art gave me comfort. Art was a friend. Art was a trusted confidant where I could escape the pain and trauma of my childhood."

'You are in the perfect place to recapture your childhood

dreams," Mauro told her. "I know some wonderful teachers where you could gain practical tuition in art."

'I don't know," she said uncertainly. "I think—"

"Don't think. Feel. What does your heart say?"

She paused. 'My heart is skipping," she said. "My heart wants to play."

"Perfecto! You have your answer. Paint the beauty of Venice. You can take some classes at the Peggy Guggenheim with internationally renowned artists I know personally."

Maggie was both terrified and excited. Nervous and delighted. Filled with fear and overflowing with joy. Maggie knew about Peggy Guggenheim. She had been a well-known American heiress whose great passion had been collecting works of art. The art museum she founded in a nearby palace was nestled along the waterways of the Grande Canal and held the most important collection of modern art in Italy. Works by Wassily Kandinsky, Piet Mondrian, Pablo Picasso, Paul Klee, Constantin Brancusi, Alberto Giacometti and other significant artists Maggie admired were all housed there.

The opportunity was beyond her wildest dreams. To study art. In Venice. With world-acclaimed artists. Liquid desire drowned her fear of not being good enough, her worry about looking ridiculous, and her anxiety about disappointing Mauro, who obviously believed in her. Mauro, who had been a stranger to her days earlier, encouraged her to nurture her more intimate passions in the most inspiring way. No one had ever done that for her.

Where would it lead? Would creativity become her new normal? And what of Mauro?

"YOU HAVE SUCH A GIFT FOR WATERCOLOURS," Mauro said when she showed him her abstract paintings of the Grand

Canal several days later. "They remind me of Turner, only more contemporary and modern. You can capture emotion. When you paint, you feel…you are not thinking. These are some of the best paintings I have ever seen," Mauro said as he thumbed through her paintings."You will be a famous artist."

Maggie almost burst into tears. "Really? Do you really think that?"

"You have the soul of an artist."

The soul of an artist.

Maggie felt a warm glow in her chest burst into fire as his words fanned over her. She was not a lawyer. She was an artist. And potentially a great one.

His encouragement meant everything to her. His belief in her gave her the confidence that she could, in time, find a new path. A path with less stress and more heart.

"Only with an artist can I have a true connection," he said.

"I could kiss you," Maggie cried.

"Go on," he encouraged.

"Here?" she said, looking at the crowds. "People will see us."

"This is Venice," he said. "No one cares."

And then he kissed her.

THAT NIGHT AFTER MAKING LOVE, they lay side by side, sharing Mauro's headset and listening to his mp3 of George Winston's hauntingly romantic piano playing. There were no words to detract from the journey into their imagination made more sensuous after their love-making.

Fate had drawn them together, as though they were destined to be together.

22

Laughter coming from his mother's apartment stopped Mauro in his tracks. Impossible, she had gone to stay with her sister. And yet her voice was unmistakable. But the laughter was a relic from the past. He hadn't heard his mother laugh in years. He approached her apartment, treading carefully so his footsteps didn't disturb her. The door was ajar. Who was with her?

Then he heard the unmistakable melodic lint of Maggie's voice. His first reaction was to panic. But they were laughing. Not just laughing. They were giggling like children.

"What's going on?" he scoured the room as he entered, looking for evidence of drinking. But the crystal decanters on the antique bureau were full of amber liquid. Golden light reflected through the Venetian glass sending out a shimmering, sultry sparkle.

"Mauro, darling," his mother said. "Have you seen these?" She gestured to the watercolour sketches spread over the polished Rosewood table.

Mauro savoured the glimmering pieces awash with the

warm shimmer of romantic rouges, sandy ochres and dazzles of misty light on sparkling water.

"Aren't they magnificent? This is the Venice of my childhood. The light, the beauty, the radiance. Only they speak of the future too. A beautiful future. Where Venice is no longer in peril but is saved. See how they glow." His mother wrapped her arm around Maggie. "Oh, Mauro, where did you find such a treasure? She has the soul of a Venetian artist."

Maggie grinned. "Without Mauro's help, I never would've been introduced to Fabrício. He's taught me so much about painting in such a short time."

"*Bravo*, Mauro. *Fantastico*," his mother said, fluttering her hands in the air. Her engagement ring, a rare amber-gold diamond that had been handed down the matriarchal line, sparkled in the sun, splaying a prism of golden light over Maggie's face.

Mauro stood frozen in bewilderment. How could the two women most important to him, the two women he worried would meet in opposition, the two women poles apart in age, culture, and tradition, have come together as one?"

"I have commissioned Maggie to paint a portrait of my mother," his mother said, passing him a framed photo of his grandmother. "I want to see what magic she can do. I never had a painting of her, your father promised, but –" her voice trailed away.

"She's so beautiful," Maggie said, registering the searingly exquisite face similar to Mauro's mother. "I haven't done a portrait before. But I would love to try. As Leonardo da Vinci did, I would love to discover how to bring your beloved mother back to life."

23

———

"Ohh, I'm getting goosebumps," Chanel said when Maggie called her on Zoom that night.

Maggie was pleased that Chanel seemed genuinely delighted.

"It's so romantic," Chanel gushed. "Look at you. You're bathed in love. I've never seen you like this. You look so happy."

Maggie grinned.

"So what are you going to do?" Chanel asked.

Maggie shrugged. "I don't know. All I know for sure is that I'm tired of the loneliness. Tired of being on my own. Tired of sitting in wine bars with my single girlfriends, complaining about what a lack of talent there is out there. I want what you have. I want to have someone at my side, to lie beside, to laugh with. To make love with."

Mostly she wanted someone to share her day with her and encourage her along as she chose a new direction, one closer to her heart. Mauro had been the only person to encourage her painting and the first to recognise her talent. She worried it would be so hard for her to keep her confidence alive without him near.

She reminded herself that love was a dangerous game, aware of the ebbing flow of her self-reliance as she imagined a return to normality and life without Mauro.

But tonight, she reminded herself, she would push her fears aside and enjoy the elusive invitation Mauro had delivered. To spend an evening with him in his private apartment. Until now, he had kept her from his inner sanctum.

24

"This is magical," Maggie said breathlessly as she stepped into the reception room of Mauro's vast apartment. She recognised furnishings she had only ever seen in magazines as Mauro guided her past Moooi's giant 'horse' lamp standing watch over a small side table by Piero Lissoni.

"I have always been fascinated by beautiful things, architecture, furniture, books. Beautiful things are prepared with love. Creating something of beauty is a way of bringing good into the world. Infused with optimism, it says simply: Life is worthwhile," Mauro said, registering Maggie's delighted approval.

Antiquity and modernity merged seamlessly in a focused curation of design classics. The furnishings were both bold and brave, subtle and silent. Angelo Mangiarrotti side tables in Carrara marble, an oversized Patrica Urquiloa purple bend sofa, and Carlo Scarpa lamps were dwarfed by the dimensions of the room and melded with its original mouldings and distinctly 16th-century antiques and architectural styles.

Maggie savoured his use of traditional materials and admired how he had created something modern while honouring history. The cast of characters weaving their stories from the ancient frescos merged with the bouquet of heady floral aromas from the many scented candles sprinkled throughout the apartment. An oversized contemporary pendant light shimmered in the moonlight, creating reflection points everywhere.

If Mauro intended to seduce her with the sensuality of his private kingdom, he had succeeded, Maggie thought giddily. But she couldn't allow herself to become intoxicated. She couldn't lose her mind. She must remain sober to avoid inevitable heartache. She would be leaving Venice soon. And Mauro. For good.

"I love the wabi sabi-like imperfection and fearless modernity," she said, walking into the dining room where wallpaper, like a colossal Jackson Pollock, created a touch of contemporary magic beneath its frescoed ceilings.

"I love juxtaposing old and new with a light modern feel," Mauro said. "Everything is Italian and, where possible, mostly local, but with a nod of approval to American modern art. This is a household that appreciates multiculturalism and a not-too-serious grandeur."

"This is a whole new story," Maggie said, "I feel like I have stepped off a plane into a different world. A different era."

It's nothing like she thought it would be.

He would be.

Ostentatious sophistication blended with comforting soft-ness. She turned to study the tapestries hanging on the walls. Her eyes travelled over the naked image of Persephone, her slender arms entwined trustingly around Hermes, as the messenger of the gods and guider of souls steered her from the throne of hell to the summit of Mount Olympus—a place where she would be safe at last.

It would be so easy to surrender to a fantasy future, she censored. Dreaming of an idyllic life with Mauro in his Palazzo where she would be eternally happy.

As she turned away, she looked into his wide hazel eyes flecked with gold and blinked in surprise. He was looking at her with such earnestness. It was as though—no, she silently reprimanded. Love stories are myths, fables. . .lies.

"When I design, I like the storytelling to be honest and true," Mauro said as though reading her thoughts. She took the crystal glass of wine he handed her and cupped her hands around the goblet as he told her the narrative he had crafted around the 16th-century noblewoman Caterina de' Medici and the historical origins that informed his work.

"I wove a tale of three cities; Florence, where she was born; Paris, where she was sent to marry the Duke of Orleans, who later became the King of France; and Venice, my home-town and my ancestors. And then I wove a tale of the future, where beauty was still referred but with a light-hearted spirit of fun ingrained into the collection."

"It has such a wonderful energy," she said as the alcohol numbed her anxiety. "I feel that good times have been had here," Maggie said, aware only after she had uttered the words that the suspense-filled anticipation of the night ahead was drowning of fear of leaving.

Why had Mauro invited her? Why now, when she was so close to leaving Venice? Why, after all this time?

"It's so important, especially in the time we are living in now, to be surrounded by objects that make us smile—and people," Mauro said, gazing at her intently before gesturing to the feature wall.

It was clear that Mauro possessed a humorous streak, she thought with surprise as she looked at the wall adorned in gilded flying unicorns against a palette of carnival blue." She loved his characterful take on luxury that honoured and played with the past.

"It's like a fairytale," Maggie said as she registered the gentle melody of a violin concerto playing in the background. "The noblewoman and the king. The American and her prince."

"So now you know the real me," he said. "Do you approve?"

Maggie was utterly enchanted. It possessed the architectural heritage of surrounding palazzos but possessed an extraordinary and unique atmosphere. He had not let any decorative piece or era dominate. The balance was perfect with its timeworn patina, with lighter touches of decadence and whimsy.

"Approve? I love it!" Her voice dropped to an awed whisper she hoped was only audible to herself. "I love you."

She saw her eyes reflected in his glistening gaze. "Perhaps you would like to see the bedroom?"

25

———

As she lay in his arms after they made love that night, it occurred to her she had never felt so vulnerable. All her life, she had fought hard to be in control, to never find herself in a situation where she would have to rely on anyone else for her survival. That had been her mother's mistake. One she vowed she would never make herself. But now, here in Venice, here in Mauro's arms, she didn't know how she would survive without him.

"Is your mother beautiful like you?" Mauro asked.

"My mother's biggest mistake had been to forgo her independence for the love of a man," Maggie said, thrown by his question. "Yet when she was saddled with six children and had lost her spark, my father thought nothing of leaving her —and us."

She raked her fingers through her hair. God, why was she offloading all this? Here? Now?

"*Mia cara*, I'm sorry he did that to you."

She gulped, swallowing the sweet, honeyed taste of his sincerity.

"My father," she began, stumbling over the words so

foreign to her, "went off searching for fresher pastures. He never even spared a thought for my mother. Or the children he was leaving behind. My mother, made weak through years of subservience to his whim and fancy, was left drained and battered. With his departure, he took any last remnant of hope. She sought comfort in bottles of Gordon's gin and guzzling wine from the cask. I was the oldest and took over parenting my five younger siblings. Working hard by day in the restaurants of New York where the high and mighty ate and studying law by night, determined not to remain trapped by circumstance. I resolved never to weigh more heavily on a man than a bird."

"A bird?"

"It was something Coco Chanel once said. I liked it."

"I would never take your freedom," Mauro said.

She turned to him in astonishment. How did he know that her greatest fear was losing herself to another and being abandoned?

26

Maggie lay motionless beneath the giant velvet festoons hanging from the canopied bed. Her mind detached from her body, hovering above them as Mauro tried to kiss her.

"I am tired," she said, rolling away from him. "I just need some space."

"Space? What is this space? I do not understand. You live on the other side of the world, and now we are together, and you want space. Our time is so short, Maggie."

"That's the point," she said. "Our time is short. Holidays always end." Dreams always end.

She wanted him to give her a practical sign, something tangible she could hold onto, some signpost, reassuring her about their future.

"Do you want to stop, Maggie?"

"This won't work, Mauro. I've thought it through."

"You didn't answer my question."

"This is love in Venice. When I've gone, we'll be nothing."

"Nothing?" He flung his legs over the bed and rose to his

feet. He stood fiercely proud and defiant over her. "Your biggest problem, Maggie, is your head. You overthink with this," he said, stabbing his temple. He pressed his left palm to his chest. "But you have blocked your heart from feeling."

Fear consumed her.

"We both know this won't last."

Even as she insisted she leave, her heart felt heavy, burdened by her complicated and complex nature. The forces within herself that sought both to be free and to love deeply and those that sought to keep her safe from the tides of passion. Why couldn't she shake the feeling he was keeping something from her?

She, Maggie Green, fearless New York prosecutor, was afraid. Afraid of losing herself. Afraid of being unable to leave and return to the other life that she knew within days she must return to. Afraid of losing. Him.

She wanted to tell him, 'I do feel. That's the problem, I feel too much, and it scares the shit out of me.' Instead, she said, "I've weighed the pros and the cons and decided. My mind is made up."

He smiled sardonically. "You sound like a lawyer."

"I am a lawyer," she threw at him, realising as she spoke that it wasn't who she wanted to be anymore. It wasn't a role she wanted to play anymore. It wasn't a life that made her soul sing as the promise of life in Venice with Mauro did.

The promise?

What promise, she reminded herself. You're dreaming. But the word lingered.

"You cannot decide with anything but your heart, Maggie. I know you. I love your head, even when it's a problem for me. You don't trust me," he said.

"We barely know each other," she began.

"You're right not to trust me, Maggie."

She felt her stomach freefall.

"I should have told you before. . ."

This was not going to be good. Her chest tightened around her racing heart.

"I want to marry you."

The magic words. The sign. The promise she could hold onto reassured her about the longevity of their future. Her heart danced, then thundered to a stop. She heard the 'but' before he spoke.

"But I am promised to another woman."

The words that followed were swallowed in a tide of roaring noise. She barely heard him say the other woman lived miles away, that they barely saw each other, that there was no love between them, that it was an arranged union of two Venetian families. All she heard was her mind yelling, 'I told you so.'

"I understand how hard it has been for you to trust me, and I wanted to make it easier. I wanted to tell you the truth."

"Well, now you have. And now I will answer your question. Yes. I want to stop. I want to stop now. I want to stop forever. I wish I'd never come to Venice."

"I love you, Maggie Green. I loved you the day I met you. My mind told me to tell you about Marina, but my heart warned me. Warned me to wait. Warned me to take time. Warned me to wait for the right moment."

"And this is it? This is the moment your heart told you to break my heart?"

"Maggie, my heart told me to ask you to marry me. My heart told me to tell you the truth even though it meant risking losing you. My heart," he pressed a hand to his chest, then pushed it to hers, "belongs to you. Not her."

Maggie clutched her head in her hands. Her mind was exploding. He loved her, but he had made a promise to someone else and kept it from her. He had only told her the truth because he feared losing her. She clenched her eyes and rocked her head, trying to make order from the chaos.

"I thought I could honour the promise I made to my mother. But I can't do it. That marriage isn't right for me. I love Venice. She loves Dubai. I love history. She loves the future. I love art, music, and culture. She loves shopping, shoes and handbags. We would end up repeating the mistakes of our pasts. The mistakes our own parents made. I won't live without love. My father tried, and he committed suicide. I need to call it off before we both make a terrible mistake. I will end it with her."

Maggie didn't know what to think. All she felt was shock and overwhelming sadness. Mauro had told her his father had committed suicide. That his parents had endured a loveless marriage, and now his mother was manipulating him to do the same. She wanted to believe Mauro; instead, she felt over-whelmed and frightened. She had been a fool for love before. She would not, could not, be a fool again.

She would cut short her holiday and leave before her heart tricked her into believing they could have a future. She was a fool for believing in a new story. A fool for learning to behave as a new person until believing she could become it. An artist. A lover—a wife. She had walked through the door of unlimited possibility and found it locked.

This was love in Venice. Magical, made-up, and make-believe. And her life was in New York. Practical, concrete, and real.

End of story.

27

Venice is empty without you.

Maggie stared at his text and hid her weeping eyes behind dark sunglasses as the Vaporetto ferried her toward Piazza Roma and the airport.

As she stared at the phone Mauro had purchased for her, she remembered his face, his eyes, and how he made her feel when she was with him. Why did it feel so real?

She scrolled through her photos. Why did they look so happy?

She, fearless Maggie, had pushed him away and now was fleeing. Coward, she muttered under her breath. What's wrong with you?

"He asked me to marry him, she told Chanel, "but I said to him, 'So Mauro, what exactly is the status of you and the woman your mother wants you to marry?' Because they are practically engaged, even though they live miles away. She lives in Dubai, and he lives in Venice. And he said, 'We are more like friends, my love. Do you want to be my future?' But how could I be his future when he was weeks away from marrying someone else? How can I trust him?"

"I remember when you first called on Zoom to tell me about him," Chanel said. "You were bathed in love. I'll never forget it. I've never seen you like that. You were radiant. Besides, practically engaged is not engaged. It's not like a real promise. And he told you it's a curse that needs to be broken."

Maggie nodded numbly.

"So what are you going to do?" Chanel asked.

Maggie shrugged. "I don't know."

Why couldn't she give Mauro her heart? He had told her she had his heart, not the other woman his mother wanted him to marry. He had told her the truth. He had done nothing to disappoint her. Perhaps she had heard too many stories of foreigners trying to marry for the right to live in America. What did that matter anyway, she wondered? Nobody married forever anymore. Why not give someone a chance to start a new life in America?

As she stepped from the Vaporetto and placed her suitcases on the cobbled street, sensuous fingers laced around her hand.

A frisson of familiar warmth coursed through her.

"Mauro! How did you find me?"

"My heart tracked you," he said.

"Seriously."

He gestured to the phone he had given her that she clutched in her hands. "I tracked you."

"Why?"

"Why? This is why." He cupped his fingers around her cheeks and drew her face toward his, and kissed her.

28

"Is that what you thought?" Mauro laughed. "That I wanted a green card or what you call it? So I could live in Disneyland?"

"There's more to America than Disneyland," Maggie said. "But, yes, isn't that what you wanted?"

"No, I do not want to live in America any more than you do." Mauro stared into her eyes. "Margaret Louise Green, what I want is you. I thought you wanted me too."

"I do."

"So you will?"

"Will what?"

"Love in Venice."

"Love what in Venice?"

"Me, you impossible woman," Mauro said. He took her fidgeting hand in his, placed it gently on his chest, and pressed her palm to his racing heart. "Can you feel what I feel?"

Maggie bit her lip, looked down and studied the sunny yellow wildflowers pushing up beneath the ochre cobbled tiles.

Mauro placed his fingers gently under her chin and raised her face to his. "Maggie, you've captured my heart."

Her lips quivered, "Please, Mauro, before you say something you'll regret . . ."

"The only regret I'll ever have is not fighting for your love. For not having allowed myself to commit to you sooner." The words he'd been waiting a lifetime to say suddenly became easier. He bent on one knee and withdrew the gold silk box from his pocket.

"Maggie Green, will you love me and marry me and live with me in Venice?"

"Mauro," she gushed. The brilliance of the show-stopping yellow diamond nestled in a bed of gold silk blinded her. Tears welled in Maggie's eyes. As a girl, she had dreamed of an all-consuming love and a romantic proposal under a sunny sky. But this was beyond anything she could have possibly conceived.

"It's your great-grandmother's ring." She felt her pulse riot in rapture as, though sensing the magic that danced between, butterflies drifted forward in a magnificent cloud.

"It is cut from 150 carats to 88.88 carats, echoing the number eight, a symbolic number in my family," Mauro said. "It is the ring of eternity."

Eight, her lucky number.

"Does this mean—?"

"Si, my mother, she has given us her blessing. She accepts that the past cannot be repeated. She knows that history is cemented by a stronger future. She trusts the beat of my heart that pulses only for you. But it is not her word that is most important to me. It's yours, Maggie. Will you marry me?"

"Yes," she cried, "Yes, a million times yes."

Mauro had left no stone unturned. He had gained his

mother's blessing. She had given them her mother's ring embodying her parent's marriage, which had been a happy union. And Mauro had promised her his heart forever.

As Mauro slipped the ring on her finger, he leaned over, touched his lips to the sparkling diamond, and kissed her. Maggie sighed into the kiss she knew would last a lifetime. And now she was sure they both really understood what true love was.

It was heaven. Pure heaven.

"Do you want to stop?" Mauro laughed as they made love three months later on their wedding night.

"I don't want to stop," Maggie said, pulling him closer. "Promise me that you will never ask me if I want to stop again."

"I promise. I will never stop loving you. We will be forever, my love."

Tears pooled in her eyes, "Yes, I would love that."

They curled into each other's arms, their heart and soul merging as the Puccini violin concerto Mio Babbino Caro played in the background.

Their future had just begun. And without saying it, they both knew they would live happily ever after. All they had to do was create it together. In the magical city, they loved and where they fell in love. And best of all, their histories had become their future.

Mauro and Maggie's baby daughter was born the following Spring, nine months to the day of their wedding. They named her Isabella Rose after his great-grandmother.

Maggie continued to paint during her pregnancy. She was

overjoyed when a New York-based contemporary art advisor, Maria Bright, contacted her and commissioned large-scale works for her wealthy collectors.

A year later, she was invited to showcase her series, New Venetian Paintings, which included the works of other leading abstract expressionists. Together with Mauro and Isabella, she toured the globe showing her work in some of the best museums and galleries in the world.

EPILOGUE

Mauro bent down to the stroller and kissed Isabella's head. Then gently swept his hands over the coils of thick black hair brushing her long lashes.

"Your mummy painted these. Isn't she clever?" he said as his 14-month-old daughter stared into the vast canvas' hypnotically transfixed by the rich flow of brilliant colours.

"They are the landscapes of my mind," Maggie said, handing him a glass of champagne as she drew to his side with a wealthy new collector in tow. "This is my husband, Mauro Toffola. Mauro, this is Anwar na Hassir. Sheikh Anwar na Hassir," she corrected.

"The landscapes of your heart," Mauro corrected, taking the Sheikh's hand and shaking it warmly. They both turned to admire the kaleidoscope of abstract shapes and ancient architecture reduced to silhouetted single planes of translucent colour inspired by Venice.

"Without Mauro, none of these works would exist," she said, gesturing to the 20 paintings expertly curated and elegantly spotlighted beneath the cavernous ceiling of the Museum of Contemporary Art in Rome.

She couldn't help hide her smile as her eyes flitted along the bottom of the canvas to the red stickers that marked every piece as sold.

"My wife is too modest," Mauro said, "The talent is all hers. I merely ignited the spark. The flame of passion burst into fire with a little encouragement."

And love. Lots of love, Maggie mused as Mauro wrapped his arm around her waist. "Now, if you excuse us, I must steal my favourite two women away. We must journey to Milan for the opening of her next show."

"You're a lucky man," Anwar said. "I possessed a love like yours once," his voice trailed away, pooling in sadness. "But I'm feeling inspired again," he said, his voice lifting. "These paintings have woken something in me. And I am excited to add all of your wife's paintings to my collection. I'm sure the show in Milan will be equally successful. Before you go, might I ask," he said, turning to Maggie, "What was the inspiration behind the series other than your love of Venice, and your husband, of course?"

"The power of art to make the world happier," Maggie said, gladdened her paintings had made such an impression on a man who clearly had experienced great sadness. "And the power of art to tell new stories. Stories about Venice and the people who love her. Stories of the power of beauty to assuage pain. Stories of the way art can conquer fear and love can triumph."

As she spoke, Isabella giggled and squealed with delight. Maggie lifted her from her stroller and held the exuberant child to her heart."The collection was inspired by new beginnings and the promise of a future full of joy. I hope these paintings bring all these things into your life too."

"Isn't she a darling?" Maria Bright, the art advisor who had discovered Maggie, gushed as she stood beside them, exchanging air kisses and handshakes. "A remarkable collection —one that can only appreciate in value," she gushed as her gaze drifted to the vast abstract landscape Maggie had painted running the length of the far wall. "Don't you just love the glints of gold, the giant expanses of canvas stained with magenta and turquoise, dancing like prisons of light across the wash of cerulean blue? The works are so rich in colour, the imagery both mysterious and elusive in the treatment of the forms."

"The colours are not really pretty. They are exquisite and full of surprises," Mauro added. "Like my wife. Layered with subtle variations and memories of things seen and loved. Each painting creates its own atmosphere of love and infinite potential."

"The collection is a tour de force, a canvas full of joy," Anwar agreed, turning to Maria. "I'm so delighted to meet your artist."

Artist.

Maggie beamed. She never tired of hearing that beautiful word. She felt so grateful—to Mauro, who encouraged her, and Maria, who had rapidly become one of her most ardent promoters.

"I'm glad Maria insisted that I visit the collection in person rather than purchase the paintings solely on her recommendation. And I'm glad she discovered you," Anwar said.

"I'm glad you did, too, because you're helping me support my special cause—I donate proceeds from my sales to help the homeless gypsies find homes and provide for their families."

Anwar smiled his approval as his gaze rested on the painting Maggie had entitled, Sunrise over Santa Maria della

Salute, a silhouette of dreams suggested by flourishes of spontaneous sunny yellows.

"The resulting images are as much concerned with the living city as it is the past and its future," Maggie explained. "It's the city of dreams. I wanted to tell a new story. The story of past glory and lost love resurrected."

"The greatest artists yield up something of themselves instead of merely reflecting back the surface of the beauties that inspired their work," Mauro said, studying the portrait Maggie had painted for his mother of her own mother. "What Maggie has created here is a profound fusion of reality with a deeply personal response—and in this lies her genius."

His grandmother's portrait with her story to tell hummed with seductive appeal. Her dark exotic eyes appear to brighten, her soft carmine lips curved into a whisper of loving approval. Below the portrait, a sign with the words "Private Collection" marked the painting as clearly not for sale.

Mauro lifted her hand and pressed his lips to Maggie's fingers, lingering over the gold wedding band nestled below the sparkling gold diamond his great-grandmother had once worn. "Fairer dreams never floated past a poet's eye."

"I'd need more of these—these dreams," Anwar said. "I'd like to commission some works. Huge in scale—for my palaces around the globe."

Maria grinned. "I can help you with that," she said as Maggie, Mauro, and Isabella bid farewell.

After the debut showing in Rome, they travelled in Mauro's private jet to Milan, where they stayed with his good friend Milanese fashion house leader Massimiliano Balforni and his New Zealand-born wife, Issy Riley.

They had such fun, and Maggie got on so well with Issy,

who was also an artist. It was hard to leave, but it helped to know that following exhibitions in Madrid, Berlin, Amsterdam, Brussels, Paris, and London, they would visit Mauro's friend Sheikh Tariq na Hassir and his wife, Melanie, who was an architect. She wondered if he was related to her new collector, Anwar.

She loved that Mauro had so many exciting and successful creative friends and how proud he was of how Maggie's art career was flourishing.

Maggie couldn't wait to see the fantastic buildings Melanie had designed in the desert Kingdom and for Isabella to meet Tariq and Melanie's children and enjoy the animal sanctuary that she had heard so much about. Maggie knew Isabella would love meeting Noor, the orphaned baby giraffe Tariq had rescued and now had her own babies. She would love those beautiful animals with hearts almost as big as Mauro's.

Maggie was happy to hear that the woman Mauro's mother had once wanted him to marry was now engaged to a Sheikh. She didn't mind that she would join them from Dubai for part of their holiday because she knew they had always been good friends and that Mauro's love for Maggie and their daughter was unbreakable.

A month later, Maggie, Mauro and Isabella returned triumphantly to New York with a massive show at the Museum of Modern Art. As they boarded Mauro's private jet to return to Venice, Maggie reflected on how much love and creativity had changed all their lives.

Like Maggie, Mauro's friends had all left behind the story they told about their pasts. They had all done the work needed to open their hearts. They had all allowed themselves to be vulnerable and to have the courage and conviction to believe in a new story. And they all learned how to behave as new people, people in love with each other, their careers and their lives, until reality caught up and their dreams came true.

Painting had freed her. Painting had released her. Painting had liberated her. But it was Mauro and Isabella who had given Maggie eternal love.

* * * * *

THE END

NOW IN AUDIO

Love In Venice is available as an audiobook for your listening enjoyment. Listen to a free sample and grab your copy from your favourite online retailer or library.

EXCITING NEWS!

In August 2023 I received the thrilling news that *Love in Venice* is a finalist in Romance Writers of New Zealand Koru awards, recognising excellence in romance writing! Readers around the world judge this award. Thank you!

AUTHOR'S NOTE

This story was sparked by several of my many visits to Venice. I have always loved my time there and have so many beautiful memories. On one visit, I was lucky enough to build a friendship with a violinist and an Italian architect who also had a wonderful antique gallery, which was his hobby and passion. I stayed in his home near San Marco in a special apartment he kept for tourists.

One evening I was invited to enjoy a meal with his mother. It was wonderful and so beautiful. The dining room was decorated with rich fabrics on the walls, and the tables were decorated with the finest china, silver cutlery and crystal glasses. His mother spoke no English but was so kind and gracious—we spoke with our eyes and smiles—the language of love. Love of cultures. Love of excellent food. Love of sharing and friendship. I have never forgotten my time with them both.

This is one of the first love stories I ever tried writing. I was initially deterred from finishing this story by some 'nega-tive' but no doubt 'encouraging' feedback that this story would be better suited to mainstream fiction rather than Mills and Boon. So this book is a little different in flavour from some of my other romances.

Now, some 20 years later, and with many novels directly preceding the publication of this book, I wanted to finish *Love in Venice* and Mauro and Maggie's love story to be shared in the way I wanted to tell it. As always, art and architecture play a beautiful role.

Venice was and will always be in my heart. I hope this story, *Love in Venice*, captures this.

If you'd like to learn more about these characters, gain inside tips into the writing process, or be the first to know when a new book is released, subscribe to my newsletter here: http://eepurl.com/cigEsH. Please email me, and I'll be in touch personally—I promise…mollie@molliemathews.com.

Did you enjoy meeting Maggie's friend and motivational life coach, Chanel Zest? If you did and enjoy romantic comedy, you'll love *Sex With Strangers*.

Sex with Strangers is a clean romantic comedy, full of quirky humour, with a few spicy bits and the promise of a happily ever after.

Read to the end to enjoy more of Chanel's story and the first three chapters.

P.S. I also thought it would be fun to weave in a few of my characters from my other stories (Tariq and Melanie from *Claimed By The Sheikh* and Massimiliano and Issy from *The Italian Billionaire's Christmas Marriage*!)

You can also meet Sheikh Anwar na Hasir in *Stolen By The Sheikh. Due for release in 2023*

THANK YOU

Thank you for reading *Love in Venice*… I hope you loved it. If you did…

1. Help other people find this book by writing a review
2. Signup for my new releases email to find out about the next book as soon as I release it, sign up here http://eepurl.com/ghM501
3. Email me at mollie@molliemathews.com with a copy of your honest review and let me know if you'd love to join my dream team and of advance readers
4. Follow me on BookBub: https://www.bookbub.com/authors/mollie-mathews
5. Stay in touch on Facebook: https://www.facebook.com/molliemathewsnz
6. Follow me on Twitter: https://twitter.com/Molliemathewsnz

7. Be inspired on Pinterest: https://nz.pinterest.com/molliemathews and Instagram: https://www.instagram.com/molliemathewsauthor

8. Follow my blog: https://www.molliemathews.com/category/blog/

9. Watch me read from my books on Youtube: MolliemathewsYouTube

ACKNOWLEDGMENTS

A huge thank you, to JoAnne W. for picking up a few pesky errors. I do appreciate the time you put into this for me. I'm so sorry you didn't get to take some time away together doing something nice instead of hubby feeling sick with Covid. I do wish this would all end. I bet you do too. It is winter here and beastly and everyone is feeling so sick. My mum is in hospital and my daughter has been too…oh, to be in Venice… but watch those gypsies! I too, was warned…and nearly got into a car driven by 'pretend' taxi drivers.

My sincere thanks also to Jan Z. who picked up a few plot inconsistencies and graciously agreed to check my revised version.

I am truly indebted.

Love Mollie

P.S. Are you curious about Maggie Green's friend and health professional Dr Elizabeth Buckley. Read more about her journey from stressed out, disillusioned health practitioner to cowboy rodeo lover in *Montana Dreams*. Coming Soon!

AND FINALLY...

Thank you for purchasing and reading my books. You are more than my livelihood—you let me live my passion. Without your love of romance and belief in the power of love, this book would never have been born. I really hope you loved *this story* as much as I enjoyed writing it. Here's to an extraordinary level of love and happiness in all our lives.

With love,

First Published 2022

First New Zealand eBook and Paperback Edition 2022

Cover Design: © Steven Novak

ISBN eBook: 978-0-9951345-9-1

ISBN Print: 978-0-9951346-0-7

Published by

Blue Orchid Publishing

New Zealand

Visit www.molliemathews.com to read more about all our books and to buy them. You will also find features, author interviews and news of author events, and you can sign up for e-newsletters so that you're always first to hear about our new releases.

❀ Created with Vellum

ABOUT THE AUTHOR

MOLLIE MATHEWS writes fun, sophisticated, passion-filled contemporary romance. She is known for her "sensual, beautiful, empowered stories enveloped in true romance" (5-star review). Her books have resonated with a global audience. She has been featured in magazines, television, and radio.

A former child and family therapist Mollie passionately believes in the power of romance to transform people's lives. She loves Mother Theresa's words, *"We are all pens in the hands of a writing God sending love letters to the world."*

Her stories are unashamedly positive, optimistic, full of fun and passion.

She is graduate of Victoria University, in Wellington, New Zealand and has given keynote speeches at romance writers conventions and international seminars.

Mollie follows the sun, dividing her time between New Zealand and exotic locations—wherever she intends setting her next romance novel. She lives with her very own romantic hero, Lorenzo—tall, dark, terribly handsome and fluent in Spanish!

Follow her on BookBub https://www.bookbub.com/authors/mollie-mathews and on her blog https://www.molliemathews.com/category/blog/ and sign up for Mollie's newsletter at www.Molliemathews.com and receive her FREE gift.

BY MOLLIE MATHEWS

GEMSTONE BILLIONAIRE BRIDES:

THE ITALIAN BILLIONAIRE'S CHRISTMAS BRIDE

THE ITALIAN BILLIONAIRE'S SCANDALOUS MARRIAGE

GEMSTONE BILLIONAIRES 2 BOOK-BUNDLE BOX SET

GEMSTONE BILLIONAIRES 3 BOOK-BUNDLE BOX SET

PASSION DOWN UNDER:

MARRIED BY CHRISTMAS
BRIDE OF GOLD
LOVE ALL OF ME

TRUE LOVE:

FLIGHT of PASSION
CLAIMED by THE SHEIKH
SEX WITH STRANGERS

***PASSION DOWN UNDER SASSY SHORT
STORIES:***

FINDING A HUSBAND
TWIST OF FATE
LOVE ME FOREVER
LOVE ME AS I AM
FOREVER AND ALWAYS
THE LIGHTKEEPER'S LOVER
*PASSION DOWN UNDER 2 BOOK-BUNDLE
BOX SET (Books 1 & 2)*
*PASSION DOWN UNDER 3 BOOK-BUNDLE
BOX SET (Books 1, 2 & 3)*

EXCERPT: SEX WITH STRANGERS

MOLLIE MATHEWS

Sex With Strangers

PRAISE FOR SEX WITH STRANGERS

"I absolutely enjoyed this story. I loved the storyline, I loved the characters, I loved the humor. I couldn't put it down. The descriptions were perfect.I loved everything about this book especially the humor. It was funny, sad at times, and I loved it."

~ Patricia Quinn

"At times playful and other times very steamy, Sex with Strangers was an interesting read. There are steamy between the sheets moments and elsewhere even if some are only in Ruby or Chanel's imagination! Chanel is definitely an x-rated life coach if only to get her best friend back in the dating game and more!"

~ JoAnne Weiss

"This is a one-of-a-kind full range of emotion book that if you have ever gone through a divorce and had a wonderfully supportive but definitely zany friend to get you through it all, you will relate to much of what Ms. Mathews has Ruby experience! There were times I laughed, times I cried, and other times I was cheerleader number one for Ruby to get her mojo on and take back her life! I wasn't a big fan of Chanel initially but even though her advice sometimes came out of left field, you realize it all stemmed from love for her friend and she just wanted Ruby to have a fulfilling relationship and be happy. I absolutely loved all the in-her-head comments that Ruby would have whenever Chanel would throw out one of her wacky life-coach do's and don'ts! Priceless!! A little more depth and development of the men that become involved with Ruby would have been nice, but that was my only real criticism. Basically, a very good book."

~ AMF

"A really good, hip, fun book. It was a riot. Great fun!"

~ Robyn Donald

"I thoroughly enjoyed it. Just lovely."

~ Daphne Claire

ABOUT THIS BOOK

In love, the most dangerous enemy is saucy secrets

44-YEAR-OLD RUBY EVANS doesn't want to be a 'leftover girl.' But finding a 'forever' man is proving impossible.

Suddenly single after 20 years of marriage, her husband is the only man she has ever slept with. But the one bit of security she always thought she'd hold onto for the rest of her life is brutally ripped from her.

Humiliatingly and cruelly ex-ed when her husband trades her for a younger model, Chanel Zest, a long-time friend and motivational life coach, comes to her rescue. Together they embark on a quest to reclaim and rebuild Ruby's shattered life and begin the gruelling process of dating again.

ONCE IN A PINK MOON, **Ruby has to play dirty...**

. . .

IF YOU LOVED Brigette Jones's Diary and enjoy romantic comedy, you'll love *Sex With Strangers*.

Full of quirky humour and the promise of a happily ever after.

Sex with Strangers is a clean romantic comedy with a few spicy bits.

1

GET A LIFE COACH

New York, December, 2005

People start over all the time. Why can't I?

My friend Chanel's a life coach here in New York. She's one of the best. She even has her own column in *The New Yorker.* Chanel has generously offered to help me. To be honest I really think I'm beyond help.

11 months ago my husband, Jon, left me for a younger woman and now they're having a baby. A baby! My life is a walking cliché. It's no wonder I'm still feeling lost, betrayed and empty. When Chanel turns up at my place unexpectedly, she tells me she thinks I have abandonment issues. No kidding! It's 3 pm on Sunday and I'm still in my pyjamas, sprawled out on the sofa devouring romance novels.

"What on earth are you reading, Ruby?" she says, screwing up her nose. She picks up several paperbacks from the stack beside the sofa. "*The Virgin Bride*? As if! *Husband For Hire?* Why bother? Why on earth are you feeding your head with this stuff?"

"Princess Diana read Barbara Cartland novels and she married a prince," I say crossing my arms defensively.

"Yes, and how did that work out for her?" Chanel asks.

With my left foot I carefully slip Joan Lust's recent novella *Cuddle Up With A Prince* under the sofa. "Besides, they're not mine," I lie. "They're Millie's. I figured seeing as I'm not getting any romance I may as well read about people who are."

"These aren't your daughter's," Chanel says tossing the books back on the sofa. "J.K. Rowling is more her bag. You'd be better off reading books about wizards and magic than you would this stuff. People who *can*—date, and people who *can't* —write about it," she says dismissively. "Reading these— these fairy tales is not going to help."

I want to tell her that reading love stories helps hugely. That reading romance makes me feel less lonely. That reading romance lets me escape. That reading romance gives me hope. But I don't bother.

"The truth is you fear abandonment and this explains your reluctance to start dating again," Chanel continues. "Think Meghan Markle."

I stare at her blankly.

"What would her life be like if she clung onto her dead-beat ex?"

"Crap."

"Exactly. It's time you went looking for a new husband," Chanel says when I confess I haven't been out for months.

Well, that's not strictly true of course. Every weekday I go to my job in a towering office on Fifth Avenue where I work as a trainee public relations adviser for The Miss America Pageant. Believe me, there's a lot of work to do as we work to rebrand the organisation. But I love that finally women are being appraised on more than big boobs and hairspray. And, after, the mass exodus of lewd members of the leadership team, finally, women are running the show.

I have other non-paid jobs too. Like walking my dog Snoutts in Central Park and running Millie, my fifteen-year-old daughter, around.

"I don't have time," I lie. "Besides I'm quite happy sitting here at home. Honestly," I protest, picking the anchovies off last night's pizza.

"Nonsense," she snaps as she brushes the dog hair from her expensive skirt. "Every woman needs a man. Especially you, Ruby."

I mumble through a mouthful of cold pizza, "But I'm enjoying my spare time—reading books, doing what I want, not having to race to get my make-up on before my husband got up and saw the real me. You don't care what I look like though do you, Snoutts?" I say, reaching down and patting the Dalmatian-cross I rescued from death-row.

Snoutts looks up at me adoringly.

I'm lying of course. The truth is I'm miserable. I miss my husband. I shouldn't after what he did, but I do. I miss being married. I miss having someone make decisions with me and dealing with things I don't want to, like taking the rubbish out and doing our accounts.

Actually, I miss sex the most. We had great sex, even after 18 years and 13 days. What if I never have sex again! That's my greatest fear. I don't know how I would even begin to meet a man, let alone have sex with a stranger.

"It's easy when you know-how," Chanel says. "Not only am I the queen of dating but in my professional role I've helped masses of women reclaim their sexual freedom."

I wish I had her self-esteem I think as I look at her. Chanel isn't the world's greatest beauty. She's got a prom-inent Jewish nose that would give Barbara Streisand a run for her money. But she has charisma like Jeff Bezos has money. She only has to walk into a room and men practically trip over themselves.

I've always admired the carefree way she flicks her vibrant orange hair, smiles demurely, and regales men with a mix of witty banter and sexual innuendo. I don't think self-consciousness even exists in her vocabulary. She wears clothes that leave little to the imagination, though she's not exactly Twiggy.

"I'm voluptuous, darling. Voluptuous. Men love women with curves," she says proudly.

I know her real secret, though, it's her confidence. I'd do anything just to have a smidgen of it. It's hard to feel confident when your husband's done a runner.

Chanel's also an expert when it comes to breaking up. From what I can remember she's never dated any man for longer than three weeks, and women pay her hundreds of dollars just for an hour of her time, eagerly drinking the wisdom she dispenses and coming back for seconds.

She's promised to give me her top get-over-a-break-up-quick tips. I tell her plenty of people have been giving me dating advice. It's just left me confused.

"A guy at work told me 'the best way to get over a woman is to get under another,'" I tell her.

Chanel rolls her eyes and groans. "Men have a different way of working through their grief, darling."

I tend to agree. For starters, everything I've gleaned from scanning men's magazines suggests they don't have an issue having sex with strangers.

"I can't imagine stripping off and being naked with anyone other than my husband," I confide. "Maybe the reason men are so untroubled is because there's a worldwide shortage of eligible men."

"Don't let statistics scare you," she says, when I tell her that in New York, women outnumber men three-to-one.

"That's not what scares me," I say. "For over 18 years my husband was the only man to see me naked. We always had sex with the light off. What if I meet someone who's into. . . well, you know, kinky stuff like doing it with the light on, or in car parks in broad daylight? I've read about things like that."

Fear clamps my stomach. "God, I couldn't bear it. They'd only have to see my stretch marks and my rolled-up tummy and they'll do a runner, too. My belly still hadn't bounced back," I say, pressing my palms firmly on my stomach. "In fact, the only thing it does is bounce."

Chanel's finger rests on her lips as though she is savoring diplomacy. "Breaking up is hard to do, Ruby. Everyone knows that but crying over spilled milk isn't going to bring him back," she says, her voice thick with intensity.

"I think 18 years of marriage is a bit more than a puddle of milk, Chanel."

"It's a figure of speech, Ruby. Of course, I *am* sensitive to the fact that you've been together a long time, but to be honest, you are rather dragging out the healing process."

She crosses to the shelf over the fireplace and picks up several framed pictures of Jonathon and me on our wedding day.

"Hanging on to happy-couple photos is definitely not the way to go. Never let yesterday consume today, Ruby." Chanel strides to the mahogany sideboard at the end of the room and throws the photos in the bottom drawer.

As she closes the drawer I fight back tears. Perhaps Chanel is right, hanging onto memories only pulls me back into a past that is no longer my future.

"If you can help me get over the humiliating fact that my

husband abandoned me for another woman and got his PA to send me a text confirming my marriage was over, you're a miracle worker. I just can't let go. I just can't move on. I just—"

"You just want your old life back," Chanel says, finishing my sentence. "Never gonna happen."

The truth knifes through me, jolting me to a stop.

"The text thing was pretty low. I know, darling. I feel it. But don't worry. Have faith. Life is about to get a whole lot better. I *am* a miracle worker," she says confidently. I hear that from my clients all the time. Trust me, darling. Before long you'll be thanking that vixen for taking him off your plate."

"Somehow I doubt that." I gaze nostalgically at the mahogany sideboard, then turn to her and force a smile. "Still I'm willing to be convinced."

"I'm going to share a few of my miracle cures with you. Are you ready for number one of my hot tips? "

I nod enthusiastically. Chanel's passion for her work and life is infectious. I've never, ever seen her down despite the fact that life has dealt her some pretty tough cards. I knew her when she was Zelda Abromovich. She changed her name to Chanel Zest when she was twenty. Chanel after her muse Coco Chanel, she told me, and Zest to better reflect her personality.

It all sounded plausible at the time but I knew the real reason was that she wanted to emancipate herself from her past. I wouldn't mind being able to liberate myself from my entire family—but we'll get to that later.

Chanel's come a long way since those troubled days. I figure if she can reinvent her life after all she's been through then she can help me too.

"Start keeping a journal. It's a wonderful way to start your day," she continues enthusiastically. "Early each morning pour out your feelings onto the page. Empty the horrible stuff out of your head onto paper, then write some positive intentions about how you want to feel. This will free you up and allow you to enjoy the rest of the day. I promise you."

"Hmm, sounds wonderful," I say, nibbling my nails. "I'd love to stop going over and over and over all the things that I must have done wrong to make Jon leave, and wondering about all the ways I could've have tried to make him stay. Things like if only I'd dressed more sexily, given him blow jobs—"

Chanel thrusts her hands in the air. "Stop! Blow jobs don't determine a happy marriage."

"According to Barbara Cartland they do," I say glumly. "She says that's why Charles left Diana."

"*Camilla* is why Charles left his marriage," Chanel says firmly. "Cheating spouses are why marriages end."

"Perhaps if I hadn't been crabby when I had my period or been more understanding when his favourite team got thrown out of the World Cup. Or if, let's be really honest, Chanel, if I'd be younger."

"You've got to stop with the terrible self-talk, Ruby. Do you have any idea what power your words and thoughts have over you? What are you feeling in your body right now?"

"In my body?" I look down at my chest and then my feet. All I can see is Mickey Mouse running up and down my flannel pyjamas. "I've got no idea. It's not saying anything to me. Should it be?"

"Your body is your temple, Ruby. It speaks to you all the time. You just haven't been tuned into it before now. Notice what your body barometer does when you start going on and on and beating yourself up like that. It makes you feel depressed, doesn't it, darling? No wonder when you start affirming that kind of rubbish. *If only. If only.* I only you would start saying some kind, loving thoughts about yourself. Try it and see what happens."

Screwing up her nose Chanel picks up the remaining pizza and gives it to Snoutts who looks at it with disinterest. "Getting rid of that processed food would help too. It's not even really suitable for the dogs," she says turning back to face me. "Now, tell me right now five things that are great about you."

"Um. . .er . . ." I trawl through my memory bank and draw a blank. "Gosh, you'll probably think I'm a real sad-sack but I can't even think of one. You don't think I'm a lost cause, do you?"

"Of course I don't, darling. No judgment, Ruby. It's quite, quite normal. You wouldn't believe how often people struggle to think of anything nice to say about themselves. You do know there's a global self-esteem virus? Why else would so many people be popping Prozac?"

I avoid Chanel's gaze and wonder if I should be canceling my prescription of antidepressants.

"Well, there's your first bit of homework," Chanel says. "Keep two journals. One for recording all the sad-sack stuff —things like how you're feeling, times when you feel blue, angry, etc. Then get yourself a fun, funky journal. We'll call it the passion journal. Start collecting positive things people say about you, and record things that inspire you or make you feel good."

Chanel reaches into her bag and pulls out a small spiral-bound notebook. "Here's your first bit of feedback."

She rips out a page, and hands it to me, along with her favourite citrus-orange Shaeffer fountain pen. "Write down what I am about to say and then transfer it to your passion journal. *You are a kind, generous, loyal, intelligent and resilient woman."*

The pen crawls across the page. I feel like such a fraud. Tears bleed across my eyes as I write each word. But then I start to feel better. I hadn't realised how much I needed to hear someone say something nice about me.

I stand up and give her a hug. "I don't think anybody has said anything quite so nice to me in a very long time."

"I'm sure they have, darling. But words are like photos—unless we record positive memories we forget them. It's amazing how memorable criticism is though. Which leads me to my next top tip for getting over a break-up fast. Learn how to meditate. Meditation is the biggest thing since gluten-free bread."

"I don't know, Chanel. I really don't think I could handle shaving my head and I can't see myself wearing a yellow robe any time soon either."

"Don't be silly, Ruby. You don't have to go all weird and new age to meditate. Just saying some simple things over and over is enough."

"Like what?" I ask her.

"Like baaaa, lamb, sheep. . ."

"Sounds pretty weird to me, Chanel."

"I'm joking, silly. But the truth isn't too far away. Any word can be a mantra. Mastering the art of meditation is simply disciplining yourself to repeat the same word over and over again. By concentrating on only one thing you can gradually silence the thousands of random thoughts that are spinning around and around in your head."

Saying one thing over and over sounds easy enough. I decide to try meditation tomorrow. I'm keen to start feeling better and Chanel must know what she's doing because she's the life coach and has qualifications coming out her ears.

"The next tip is fabulous, darling. I know you're going to love it. Eat loads of chocolate ice-cream," she suddenly looks serious. "The ice-cream has to be *Mövenpick.*"

I'm starting to wonder about Chanel. Her advice doesn't sound very normal. But then Chanel is quite possibly the zaniest person I know. I do like ice-cream, and *Mövenpick* is exquisite.

"The next tip is in the same box as getting rid of photos," Chanel says.

I brace myself.

"Delete lovey-dovey emails, bin the heart-wrenching texts and burn old love letters."

I bite my lip pensively. I'm a romantic at heart and asking me to throw away my love letters is like asking Linus or Baby Bop to throw away their comfort blanket.

I'm not sure if I'm ready for this.

"Hanging onto old emails is seriously bad relationship feng shui," Chanel insists. "Change the energy flow in your home, darling. Change your life."

"It sure would be great if all I had to do to get over Jonathon was press delete, and whammo he would be gone," I say.

"Believe me it is," Chanel says. ". . . that and dating and time. Of which, might I say, I think you've had quite enough. Grieve any longer than 11 months and you'll head down the slippery slopes of depression. Believe me, that's the last thing you want. It's a steep climb once you've plummeted. Besides, you don't want Jonathon to think he's won, do you?"

I shake my head.

"Good. I can tell you, both as your friend and life coach, that there is no way I'm going to let that cheat come out of this break-up better than you."

I suddenly feel self-conscious sitting around in my pyjamas. Perhaps *I am* sliding toward the icy slopes of depression.

"I guess I can store my letters at my parents and retrieve the emails back from the trashcan if I don't feel better," I whisper tentatively.

Chanel's brows furrow into a scary frown. "What's the point of holding onto them?" Chanel says impatiently. "They're only words. Words from the scum that left you for another woman."

Ouch, that hurts. But it's true. I resolve to push delete as soon as I get to work.

"The next tip is a no-brainer but you'd be surprised how frequently people don't realise how unhelpful some of their friends can be. To really move forward it's important to surround yourself with friends who make you laugh. Friends who will introduce you to other single men."

"Other than you, Chanel, I can't think of anyone. Most of my friends were Jonathon's friends and those who have stuck with me don't laugh anymore. They're working ninety-hour weeks and are so stressed out that all they do is come home and blob out in front of the telly. Gosh, now that I think of it that's why so many of my girlfriends are like me—shagless and single. As for my married friends— well, it turns out they weren't really my friends at all."

"It's incredible how invitations to dinner parties dry up when you're single and dateless, darling," Chanel says.

"I know. And when I did go to a few I got the distinct impression some of the women thought I was threatening. As if! To be honest," I say, "I just end up feeling miserable. They're married and *I'm not.*"

"Which brings me to the next rule. Stay away from married friends." Chanel wags a manicured finger at me.

"And stay well away from anyone who looks even the teeniest bit like they might get married."

"Okay," I mumble.

"Definitely don't go to any weddings. You'll only get stuck on the singles table, and believe me," she says solemnly, "that's dating suicide."

"Really? I thought that would be a great way to meet someone."

Chanel lowers her chin and looks at me over the bridge of her nose, "Are you kidding me? Only the desperate go to weddings on their own. Far better to buy a date rather than go it alone. Desired people are desirable," she says. "Which leads nicely into tip seven: *Be glad that you were loved and that you had that person in your life.* Some people live their whole lives never being loved."

I sniffle as tears loom again. "I was glad. Really glad. I was happy loving my husband. I thought he'd be in my life forever."

"Don't be silly, Ruby. That's irrational," she says, handing me a tissue. "Nothing lasts forever. But," she says, her voice softening, "tip eight is relevant here: give it time. Grief does have its own sense of timing."

This doesn't sound like Chanel. "Are you sure?" I ask uncertainly, wiping my eyes.

"Just don't grieve too long. No one likes a sad-sack."

That sounds more like Chanel.

"On that note, and concluding today's lesson, is tip nine: find some fun! Book a holiday. Have a makeover. Spoil yourself rotten. Have something to look forward to or do whatever gives you a buzz. Which leads me to the next point," she says, reaching into her bag. "I've got just the cure. Do you remember my cousin Julie?"

"The pretty one who left her husband and ran off with a surf instructor from Malibu?"

"She did? Oh yes. . .that was ages ago. A year at least. She's been single since then and having a fantastic time. But we're keen to take our loving offshore and have some European fun. We're already booked," she says, passing me a travel brochure, "and the best part is, there's room for you!"

I take the brochure tentatively and thumb through it before returning to the cover page and reading, *Contiki for 18-35s. European Inspiration Tour: 19 days from London to Amsterdam, Berlin, Prague, Munich, Venice, Rome, Florence, Lucerne, Paris and more.* "I've always wanted to go to Europe. But Contiki? Don't you think we're getting a little old for this?"

"Don't be silly, Ruby. We're the perfect age. We're 35 -"

"We're over forty, Chanel."

"Don't say the "f" word, Ruby, it's not polite. Besides, we don't look a day over thirty. With our wisdom, experience and mature outlook on life, we know who we are and what we want. We're an asset to the young."

"We are?"

"Yes, we are! Men love confidence, and confidence comes with experience. Which Julie and I have. . . and you will soon. We've got it all mapped out, and Contiki is just the company to help us realise our dreams."

"What dreams, Chanel?" I ask nervously.

"We want sex," she replies matter of factly, "and lots of it."

"We do?"

"Absolutely. I read an article in *The New York Times* the other day that said one of the biggest regrets people had was not having enough sex. That and not marrying the right person. And you know about that already. I for one don't want to die with regrets. Do you, Ruby?"

"I guess not."

"You guess not? How many lives are you planning to have, darling?"

"Don't be silly, Chanel. Everyone knows you only get one."

"Not everybody believes that," she corrects me. "But for simplicity's sake let's assume it's true. Do you really want to use yours up crying over a disloyal prick of a husband or are you going to join our race?"

"What race?"

"Our race to conquer Europe. Julie and I have set each other a dare. We've got to bonk a guy in every city we go to. The winner gets to have fabulous sex with a bevy of European lovers.

"And the loser?"

"The loser gets to have sex—only with less strangers."

"I don't know, Chanel. This sounds a bit desperate and dangerous. I mean, gosh, we're middle-aged, and you already have a head start when it comes to picking up strange men. To be honest, it's not really my thing."

"Come on, it'll be good for you. A fresh start. A chance to sample some of the stuff you've been missing. Maybe have a fling with a younger man. Haven't you heard that old Chinese proverb about being as old as the last guy you screwed?"

"I can't say I have, Chanel. I think we must read different books."

"Yes, darling, we do," Chanel says, glaring at Joan Lust's novel stuffed under the couch. "Think of it as sexual healing, Ruby. The point is to have fun flings, not full-on relation-ships. Besides, having one night stands has been scientifically proven to boost your chances of finding love again. Not only do they broaden your sexual repertoire, but they also boost your self-esteem. And let's face it, darling, yours is pretty deflated. So what's to lose?"

"Scientifically proven?"

"Absolutely! 100 per cent guaranteed. Knowing you may never see your conquest again allows you to practice the one thing that will stand you in good sexual stead forever."

"Which is?"

"Saying what you want in bed."

For a moment I'm sure my breathing has stopped.

"I know what you're thinking. You're mortified right?"

"Have I gone a pale shade of white?" I hope my laugh sounds less self-conscious and more, *'this is going to be so much fun.'*

"Grinding your teeth together kind of gave you away," she says putting her arm affectionately around me. "Relax! Believe me—I know. Asking for what you want is the key to a happier life. One-night stands are the perfect way to practice. Oh, and news flash—sex outside of marriage is not a cardinal sin. This is the new millennium, the era of female empowerment, freedom, and choice. Don't waste your life making the wrong ones my sweet. Life's too short and too precious for that."

I do like the idea of getting away, and coming from a family of seven sisters has instilled a competitive streak in me. But racing to take European men to bed isn't exactly the same as grabbing the last potato at dinner. And everyone knows that European men are a lot less uninhibited. They're bound to want to do it with the light on.

I clench my hands over the cushions on the couch. "It's a bit of a stretch, Chanel. I mean, it's all right for the two of you —you're experienced. I wouldn't know where to start. Gosh,

I think I'd fall over if any man other than Jonathon looked at me in an amorous way."

I twist my gold wedding band. The divorce isn't finalised yet and wearing his ring still gives me comfort. It was like a neon sign telling the world someone had picked me. I was wanted.

"Don't worry, we'll get you up to speed. I'm a life coach after all. Helping people with relationship issues is my specialty."

Suddenly I'm more nervous than when Millie tricked me into going on the world's biggest, oldest, and most rickety rollercoaster. I'm half excited and half out of my mind with fear. Mostly it's fear I feel as I say, "It all sounds great. When do we start?"

Feel the fear and go dating anyway, right? Although in Chanel's hands at least I won't die.

Will I?

2

____

MID LIFE MELT DOWN

"Maybe I do need to see a counsellor after all," I say handing Chanel a tumbler filled with refreshing gin and tonic the following week at home.

It's been a hard week at work and an even harder week personally. "I think I'm having a mid-life meltdown. I know I've never had one before so it's also possible it is something else. . .but Chanel, tell me what you think. You'll know. I mean you must have seen it all before."

"Darling, I'll need more detail to make an accurate diagnosis." Chanel places the tumbler down on the glass coffee table and looks around the room. "Now where did I put my stethoscope?" Laughing, she reaches behind the cushions on the couch. "I could've sworn I left them right here when I examined my last victim. . .er, I mean client"

"I'm being serious." I walk over the stereo unit tucked away in the floor-to-ceiling bookshelves and turn the volume down. "I don't feel quite myself," I continue, turning to face her. "In fact, I feel positively glum. I just feel so confused about everything."

"Everything? Like what everything?" Her lips still smile but her eyes study me seriously.

"Like who I am and what I'm doing and where my life is going."

"Oh, that kind of everything," Chanel nods sympathetically.

"I've been trying to stay positive like you said. I've been doing the running meditation - religiously in fact. Snoutts quite enjoys it. I end up calling his name so often trying to coax him away from all the female dogs, Snoutts has become my mantra. Why they have to sniff each other's bums? I'll never know. Anyway," I say, pushing my thoughts to the issue I hope Chanel can help me solve.

"I got rid of all my old wedding photos. I binned the lot of them. Well, not quite. They're in storage. But it's close enough and you were right it was incredibly freeing. It's just. . .well, despite all your fabulous tips I still feel down."

"What are your symptoms? Hot flushes? Night sweats? Mood swings? Panic attacks?"

"No nothing like that."

"Oh, that's good. We can rule out premature menopause then."

"Oh God, I've still got that to look forward to and I'm already depressed. Depressed and in a bit of a rut. I had my whole life mapped out. I was going to age peacefully into retirement knowing that I had my man by my side. If he'd told me he wanted more, something different - well I might have tried to accommodate him. If he'd wanted a mistress I might have turned a blind eye. Like the french do. But divorce! God no."

"You've spent your whole marriage accommodating him. You deserve a sufferance medal if you ask me."

"I know you never liked him. But I did. I loved him. Now

I feel such a failure. All of my sisters, all six of them, and my parents are still happily married. Not a blemish. Then along comes me. The Black Sheep." My voice began to shake. "A blight on the family album ever since I was born."

Tears well in my eyes. "I can't seem to do anything right, as my parents so frequently remind me. And I feel stupid, so incredibly stupid. Why didn't I see it coming? Surely there were been signs. Lipstick on the collar, weekends away—"

"Jonathan's such so tight when it comes to spending money I'm sure the whole affair happened in the photocopier room in his office."

I knew she was trying to use humour to lift my soggy spirits but I couldn't even manage a smile. "I never even saw it coming. Never." My lips begin to tremble then the flood gates open. For the first time in months, I ball my eyes out.

"I wondered when you'd finally crack," she says putting her arms affectionately around me. "Have a good old cry. Better in than out. You've been a pillar of stoicism. Keeping all your feelings inside. Trapping them beneath all your layers of propriety. I understood of course. You had Millie to think of. But it's no good keeping your emotions bottled up. That's a surefire way to aid and abet that demon depression. Think about it—de-press-ion. . .you depressed all those feelings below the surface. No wonder they're breaking free now. And bloody good job. They need a good airing. Then they can jolly well bugger off."

"Do you think I'm going mad?" I sob. "I'm so afraid. Afraid I'm losing my mind. I can't sleep. I eat all the time in some sort of desperate attempt to soothe myself. Now, look at me. I look like Mrs. Blob - Miss blob,' I correct myself despondently.

"You're not going mad. Quite the opposite really. The biggest mistake people make is thinking they can go around being all jolly, jolly all the time. Quite ridiculous. You've just been through a bereavement for goodness sake. And unlike other people I could name, you took your marriage vows very seriously. Literally by the book. That's you. Always has been. When the priest said til death do you part, how were you to know that God's will would be undone by United States Law and one determined long-legged blonde? Of course, you're not naïve. You did know divorce was possible, after all over fifty percent of all marriages end up in the divorce courts, it's just you never thought it would happen to you. Why would you? Not with your family history. Unlike me. My parents separated when I was one. They never bothered to get married. I guess that must have made things easier when they split," she says bitterly.

"But hey we're not here to talk about my messed up childhood, darling" She smiles brightly, reaches into her bag, and hands me a packet of tissues. "We're here to talk about you and your mid-life blues."

"I feel terrible, obsessing about my worries. I mean, if you'd rather change topic."

"Don't be daft. Stop putting other people first. I'd much rather talk about your problems than open the lid on mine" she laughs self-consciously, "besides I'm the life coach. It's my job to listen to you. And my pleasure," she adds. "So, tell me about this mid-life meltdown of yours."

"It's just, well. . . " I bite my lip. "I feel so frumpy," I blurt. "Look at me." I lift a few locks of mousy hair. The fine strands fall limply through my fingers.

Chanel nods. "Mmm. I see what you mean, darling. This definitely isn't your best look—sort of bag lady meets Charlize Theron in *Monster*."

"Chanel!" I cry. "Do you have to be quite so cruel?"

"Well, you did ask," she replies nonchalantly. "Besides

I'm one of your biggest fans and I wouldn't have said it if I thought you were beyond hope."

"Gee thanks."

"I know that under all that limp mousy hair there's a gorgeous woman waiting to be rediscovered. Kind of like that sculptor guy. What's his name? You know the one who said he could see an angel in the block of cold marble — his job, he felt, was to set her free."

"Michelangelo di Lodovico Buonarroti Simoni."

"Ahhh. Yes, him. That guy. You always were good with names. Ohh can you imagine what that man's hands would feel like on your skin?"

"Calloused I imagine."

"Oh, Ruby you are melancholic. Michelangelo was an artist, not a labourer. I thought this sort of stuff was your passion. You always loved art at school and look at this place. It's absolutely crammed with beautiful paintings. What you need is a creative man, someone like Michelangelo. Just imagine the attention he would bestow upon you. Think about him caressing your skin, exploring your body in every minut detail, feeling his way tentatively over every muscle, every bone—"

"Every lump of cellulite," I interrupt.

Chanel ignores me and continues with her fantasy. "Imagine him peppering your body with kisses before bringing you to a shuddering climax."

I shift uncomfortably on the couch. "He's gay Chanel, and all this talk makes me feel like some creepy voyeur. But I am curious about where this is heading. How exactly are you and Michelangelo going to do to help me break free?"

"For starters, darling, this has got to go," she reaches over and lifting some strands of my hair. "Chop it. All of it."

"But it's taken me years to get it this long," I place a protective hand over my head and slide it through the ends.

"Years to end up with long, thin mousy hair? I don't know why you bothered. It only makes you look old."

Chanel wasn't the most predictable of characters but one thing I could rely on Chanel for was her honestly. And she wasn't failing me now. It is tough to hear, but I need someone strong to motivate me into action.

I start to feel excited and nervous about what she might suggest I do. Chanel has always been a bit of a glamour queen, in an out there, outrageous kind of way. Perhaps not in the style that I might want to emulate, I think as I look at her flaming orange hair.

She often wears it piled high onto her head and twisted into a top knot. Her fringe is cut short so that it almost reaches her hairline. A blonde peroxide skunk-like stripe runs through the middle of it. I get up and walk over to the mirror which hangs over the mantlepiece and study my reflection in the mirror. Drab. Drab. Drab.

"Hmm, I guess you have a point," I say, turning to her, "but no persimmon orange."

"God, no darling. Orange on you would be terrible. I wouldn't dream of it." She picks up one of Millie's fashion magazines which are sprawled over the coffee table. She licks her forefinger and thumbs quickly through the glossy pages. "What about his?" she asks, lifting the magazine and pointing to English actress Sienna Millar.

"Jude Law porked his kids' nanny and she did a Bobbitt," Chanel says. "She didn't cut off his penis, which in my book she should have, but she did cut off her hair. And now look at her. The press loves her and her career's never been healthier."

"To be honest I preferred her hair longer. Is there anything a bit less severe-looking?" I wasn't quite ready for hair that barely touched the top of my ears.

Chanel points to a photo of the singer Faith Hill sporting a new layered bob.

"Ohh, I quite like that," I say, beginning to get enthusiastic. "Did her man jilt her too?"

"Nope her hair was so badly frizzled she was left with no option." Chanel studies my hair intensely, "yours is pretty frizzled too, Ruby."

"It's stress."

"It's hardly surprising. You've had the two major stressors—make that three, in the space of one year. Separation, cheating, change of financial circumstances—oh, and career. So that's four. I'm amazed your hair hasn't dropped out completely."

I look at her with horror. "You don't think it's going to, do you?"

I could see it now. Bald, fat, and single for the rest of my days.

"Not if we act fast and give it the chop. How about a combo, darling? Let's blend a little bit of Meg Ryan's tousled just-got-out-of bed-hair, Faith Hill's sleek and sexy, and Sienna's Millar's blonde bombshell."

"Me blonde? I can't imagine it? I'll look like mutton dressed as lamb."

"Not a chance. Not with me as your creative director."

I threw her a dubious look. Stripped stockings, orange cardigan, mauve skirt—okay so they were all designer labels - but subtle Chanel wasn't. She looks more like an impressionist painting. A riot of color clashing in an orgasmic symphony.

"I know what you're thinking. But just because I dress like this doesn't mean I'm going to create a clone. This is my signature look. My brand. My statement. My *je n'est sais q'uoi.* My DNA, darling." She threw her hands around her as she spoke.

"Alright. Alright. I get it. It's your secret sauce." Secretly I envy the way she lives her life with colour. She knows how to wear clothes that suit her personality. I can't think of many people who can throw together such an eclectic array of clothing. She's like a person throwing together a salad with whatever strange ingredients are on hand and pulling it off.

"Yes, darling. One hundred and fifty percent me. I wouldn't replicate me for all the tea in china. Not even for you Ruby-do," she says giving me a hug. "Now get dressed and get ready to have ten years knocked off your dial."

"Where are we going?"

"Kenneth Amore, style queen and hairdresser to the stars."

3

GETTING BACK IN THE SADDLE

Get back on the horse, my friends tell me, but not one of them tells me how. Besides, when did being divorced by the man you thought you'd spend the rest of your life with equate with being bucked off a stallion?

"Well, for starters it hurts like hell," Chanel tells me the night she drags me out to a singles bar. "Here, take a swig of this for courage." She hands me a highball glass full of ice and a dazzling amber-coloured liquid.

Obediently I take a take a long sip. "Cripes, what's in this? My head is spinning already and I've only had a little bit.

"You always were a cheap date," Chanel giggles. "It's a Long Island Iced Tea, darling. The fun thing is there is definitely no tea in it whatsoever. Just loads of vodka, rum, tequila, triple sec and—" she turns toward the barman, "Joe, darling, what else goes in this?"

The barman flashes Chanel an alluring smile. "Half an ounce of gin, Kitty Kat." His eyes linger on her voluptuous breasts before he saunters off to the other end of the bar.

"Kitty Kat? How well do you know this barman, Chanel?"

"Intimately, darling. Intimately. Isn't he divine?"

I cast an eye over him. He's not exactly my type, but then I don't know what my type is anymore. As I check him out I begin to see what she might find attractive in him.

With his blond hair stylishly tousled, blue eyes like Robert Redford's, flawless, copper-coloured skin, chiseled jaw, and the best smile in Manhattan, Joe is handsome in a *Cleo-centerfold* kind of way. His physique more than matches his looks.

Dressed in a skin-tight white tee-shirt he has pecs to die for and a flat taut stomach that I'd give me eye teeth for. As he moves around the busy horseshoe-shaped bar I can't help but steal a look at his tight, muscular, butt cheeks. Why is it men are always blessed with the kind of bodies they desire in a woman—except, of course, for the lack of breasts.

Mortification turns my face crimson when, my eyes still riveted to the seat of his pants, he turns back toward me and winks. I thirstily gulp my drink.

"I'm glad you like the cocktail, but what do you think about the eye candy? He's more than a pretty picture—he's a blimmin' good lay too." Chanel slides her fingers up and down the straw. "Whew, it's hot in here," she says picking out a cube of ice and tracing it across her breast.

"Chanel Zest, you are wicked!"

"Wicked is the new good - haven't you heard? It's time you got a bit more wicked too, Ruby."

"I don't know, Chanel. I'm not judging you or anything, but this flirting with the ice thing and slipping and sliding with the straw. It's not really me."

"How do you know? Once you try it you might just find it's more like you than you think."

"Maybe," I say dubiously.

"Like I keep saying, getting over a break-up is like riding a horse — first you have to be willing to get on the horse, secondly you have to learn a few tricks. It's easy when you know how, especially when you have an expert rider like me to teach you. Thirdly, no one says you have to stay with one horse. It pays to ride a few before you partner up with your next stud."

"Uugghh, that's gross. Besides, I'm a one-man-woman. You know that."

"You were, Ruby. You were a one-man woman but now you're a no-man woman. I don't mean to be harsh, but you've got to face facts. He's not coming back."

"But I still love him."

"Loved him. Past tense. Any man who runs off with a two-bit showgirl like Jon did, and then sends you a text telling you your marriage is over, isn't worth loving. It's time to move on."

"I know you're right. It's just that it's so hard. Everywhere I look there are reminders of him. The waiter looks like a tad like him and now they're even playing our song."

What are the odds of a mid-town Manhattan bar playing *Love Me Tender?* Next to zero. But fate has decided today had is the day for Elvis to croon out the words which played when we were married.

"Hey, Joe, Darling, " Chanel calls out, "do you mind picking another tune. My friend's allergic to this one."

Chanel reaches into her bag and pulls out her signature pen, as Joe selects Elvis's *Hound Dog*. "Perfect choice, darling," she says to him as she slides a couple of paper serviettes toward me.

"The problem is you've romanticising him. I see it all the time. Clients are always focusing on the things they loved about their partners and conveniently forgetting the things they didn't like. It's classic Pollyanna thinking."

Chanel slips another drink to me and passes me her pen. "Do you know in all this time I've never heard you badmouth him. It's not healthy to put people up on pedestals, Ruby. More than that, it's not realistic. I want you to write down a list of all the things that you didn't like about him. Remember no one's perfect - even Jon Sugar Jnr."

"I feel mean doing this. I know he left me, but obviously I wasn't what he wanted anymore. I can't really blame him for that, can I?"

"Forget about blame Ruby, and quit with the martyr self talk too. Just write down the things you didn't like — things that if you'd had the chance you'd have liked to change. Imagine you're designing your dream man and that by writing down the things you didn't like you're getting clearer about what you want in your new husband."

"Ohh, that would be cool. I'd love it if I could just write a list of the things that I wanted in a man, send it to Amazon, and he'd get couriered to my door."

"What if I told you it is. I'll let you into a wee secret. Reality begins in your mind. Not the way we're been conditioned to believe. Your thoughts create your intentions and your intentions guide your actions and everything else flows from there. The secret my darling is the law of attraction. Start telling the universe what you're looking for in a man. Let it know what you want to attract. Come on write it down! What are you waiting for girlfriend?"

"Well, okay—here it goes. If I'm honest Jon could be incredibly domineering and bossy. Ohh, and stubborn. I've never met a more stubborn man. He was incredibly lazy too, expecting me to pick up after him all the time. I blame his mother. She over mothered him. He was way too serious as well, especially about work. He'd come home really wound up, go up to the bedroom, flick on the TV and not come out for hours."

Chanel gestures to the paper. "Write down, *uncommunicative during times of stress* and then turn it around so that you're affirming what you want, like *great communication skills even when things are difficult.*"

"Definitely!" I scrawl the words down in big bold letters across the napkin.

"Now turn the other things you said around — the last thing you want to do is attract all the things that annoyed you."

I write down, *collaborative, easy-going, flexible, and helpful.* I'd never stopped to consider what I was looking for in a man before and until I starting writing I really couldn't pinpoint what it was about Jonathan that always had me a little on edge. It felt really freeing — both naming the things that weren't right in our relationship, things that I had bottled up for years like rust that never really sleeps, but also getting clearer about what I wanted.

"Anything else?"

"This sounds silly. Promise me you won't laugh, but he had incredibly bad underwear. He always wore those horrible white Y-fronts. I never complained - I mean they were practical, and easy to soak and keep white, but not exactly sexy if you know what I mean. Yet he'd rant and rave if I ever wore beige underwear. That's the other thing. He had a terrible temper."

"You can always tell a man by their underwear, Ruby. It's been scientifically proven."

I look at her skeptically and write down, *must have great underwear — Calvin Klein or similar. Even if there's no science behind correlating men's underwear with positive personality traits I'm going to make that one of my non-nego-tiables.*

"Not a bad list, Ruby. Anything more you want to add before we file it away and get onto my next coaching intervention?"

"Wow, you're really working me hard," I laugh. "But if I could change another thing it would be the fact that he always had the TV on. I mean *always*. Boxing, baseball, sports. . .all we ever watched was the sports channel. Because I wanted to do things as a couple I sat there with him. Eventually, I learned a bit about the games but I can't say I ever enjoyed them. It would be nice to meet someone who shared the same interests as me. Someone I could talk about music and art with and maybe even go to shows with. Someone with a great sense of humour who could crack me up wouldn't go amiss either."

"Coming right up. You wait and see, Darling. Just by saying you want these things you've begun to make your dreams a reality. Happiness will come when you least expect it."

"Sounds like the Long Island Iced Teas talking."

"It takes more than two drinks to knock the sense out of me. It's like the horse scenario. You can say you want to ride a horse, even visualise it, but unless you get on the damned thing you're going no where."

Sex With Strangers *is in* paperback, ebook and audio available now from all good bookstores and libraries.

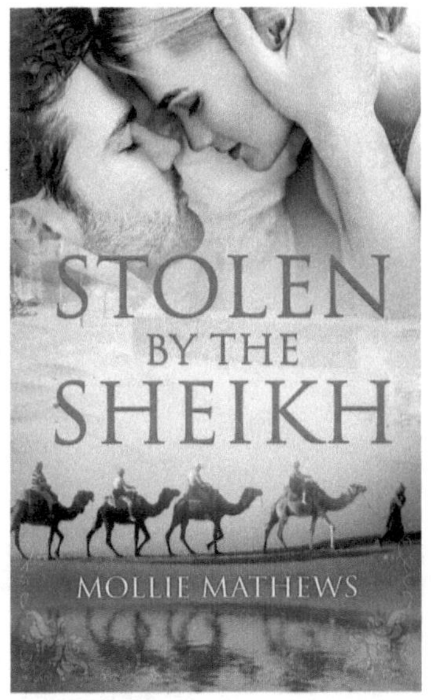

In life and love, it's never too late
for a second chance. . .

An established contemporary artist, Lucy Ford was absolutely content with her life—until the day Anwar na Hassir strolled into her gallery. A widower with two daughters, Anwar was as formidable as Lucy was freewheeling, and was both amused and appalled by her world of hedonistic, highly-strung, rebellious artists, and The Beatles, her pair of snoring cats.

But after Anwar impulsively invites Lucy to his desert Kingdom, somewhere between the magic of the desert and the stroll along the ocean, she let him steal her heart. Only to discover, love once given, can never be returned.

A sensuous tale of modern love, career-crossed relationships, the heady magic of instant attraction, loss, and the unwavering faith that sustained them—even in the darkest hour.